SITTING ON A HEADSTONE

ROBERT LAFOND

Inquiries and Book Orders should be addressed to:

Great Writers Media
Email: info@greatwritersmedia.com
Phone: 877-600-5469

ISBN: 978-1-960605-11-5 (sc)
ISBN: 978-1-960605-13-9 (hc)
ISBN: 978-1-960605-12-2 (ebk)

PROLOGUE

He wore his country's uniform at what seemed a long time ago. Now, how does he tell his children what he did in the war? That he was in a combat theater? Does he hide his uniform, hoping they won't see it, hoping to forget it? Some of his buddies said they will burn their uniforms; erasing that time in their lives when the horror, the combat was everyday life.

But they won't be able lock away the memories. They will come back through the color of their dreams, in some of the littlest things they thought was just everyday stuff. They'll blame it all on their time in the Army, the Navy, or the Corps.

Visiting friends once a week at the local tavern or the town cemetery will smother the pain for a little while. Maybe the wife has gotten used to seeing him get up early and toss off his sweaty pajamas when it's 15 degrees outside. How long will she stay by his side; holding him up like a crutch, trying to make sense of what happened, what kind of hell the war put him through at 18. He lives it still.

CONTENTS

Introduction

This story will follow the life of an 18-year-old young man, from his beginnings in a small Rhode Island town to life as a soldier on an Army base during the turmoil of the Viet Nam war. From the peace and comfort of his village life into the tormenting heat and long days of the Southeast Asia dry season. His duties in the sun will brown his back a golden tan. During the torrential downpour of the rainy season, he will curse the soil's cement-like, sticky red clay, making it a challenge to move around, even in a vehicle.

Fear will envelop him during those long nights that guard duty brings, casting doubt on his reasons for enlisting. When he is convinced that death is watching him, he will abandon that fear and place duty and patriotism before his life. He won't laugh at Death or dare it to challenge him. He won't think about it. After which, he will recognize the meaning of the phrase pervading the base, *sitting on a headstone*, and every day in Nam, and the rest of his life.

Bob Lemon comes from small-town America, where the folks in the village are good neighbors. Parents wave to each other on Sunday mornings, on their way to church. Children walk to the only elementary school, just up the hill. The children fight, and they make up. They throw snowballs in the winter and swim in the canal, aside the river, on hot summer days. He is one of those children, and like most friends, his future will go from the local elementary school to the distant high school into a predestined future. Some of his friends will go to college, while others will serve their country in the military, finding themselves fighting in a foreign land. Those thinking their high school education was enough will try to find employment through their diploma.

Others may return home mentally and physically scarred and wounded by the war in Viet Nam while others will come home locked in a vault for all eternity. The students choosing to continue protesting the war and the government would find themselves running from their obligations to seek asylum in a foreign country, carrying shame and cowardice with them the rest of their lives.

Enlistment in the US Army will be the one sure thing in Bob's future. Boot camp, helicopter mechanics schooling, and 18 months as a member of the 25th Aviation Battalion, 25th Infantry Division in the Republic of South Viet Nam. Those days will fill the most significant part of his military career. It will also be the most decisive turning point in his life. His duties as a helicopter mechanic would turn his life upside down, watching friends come and go after completing their 12-month tour of duty; others would leave after being cut short by death. The concussive reality of mortars exploding all around him will throw fear in his heart and show death at his door, again questioning his enlistment and moral obligations. His volunteerism and sense of duty to his country would put him through six additional months of combat hell, which would age him at 20 years old' and impact the rest of his life.

This story is written in a familiar, conversational way, as one would speak growing up, living with family and friends.

Any similarity between the characters in this story and individuals living or dead is purely coincidental. Place names and associations with federal or government organizations is employed for dramatic effect with no intent to harm or besmirch the name or reputation of any individual or peoples.

Sitting On a Headstone is written solely as an incomplete autobiography of the author.

CHAPTER 1

Decisive Irony

I t was two days past my 18th birthday, the age Uncle Sam required me to register for the draft. Then I received a reminder in the mail. The government was kind enough to include the penalty for not registering, so I registered. The nearest draft board was ten miles away, in the heart of Woonsocket. Mom knew the city, so she agreed to drive me there.

The draft board's office was on the second floor of a building that belonged in the last century. The stairway was a dark oak only visible by the light coming in off the street or the light at the top of the stairs. Why did it have to smell so old? There were no recruiters located on that floor, but there were plenty of giant posters of the Army, Navy, Air Force and Marine Corps. All the way down the end of the hallway was the US Coast Guard representative. It seemed lost that far down the hallway. I couldn't see it very well for the lack of lighting and the dark yellow wallpaper, torn wallpaper.

Mom and I walked into the draft board and saw a bespectacled old gentleman sitting behind a very large roll-top desk. He seemed so lost behind it. He stood his six-foot frame up and offered a friendly welcome.

"You've come to do your duty, young man?"

"Yes, sir. I need to register for the draft. I just turned 18 a few days ago."

"And you brought your mother with you," the old man said. "Well, it's nice to have that kind of back up when the courage starts to falter." He pulled a couple forms out of his desk and had me fill them out. There were flyers on a desk from the Army, Navy, Air Force, and Marines, with enticing pictures of snappy uniforms and action-filled adventure. The old man told me the recruiters come in every morning to make sure there is a supply of flyers for every young man that walks into the office. When I was finished, he had me raise my hand and swear, "I, Robert Lemon, due solemnly swear…" to the validity and truthfulness of the information I put on the sheet. I asked the old man, "Who would lie on a government form?"

"Some do, son, some do," he told me. "But they get caught in the end."

We said goodbye and thanked the gentleman as I picked up one of each of the pamphlets to bring home to my little brothers. I would scan through them earnestly that night hoping to get a clue of which Service might be best for me. I needed to keep Uncle Sam from grabbing my ass by lottery and sending me off to war post haste. There were programs in the military that would include guaranteed schooling in particular fields. I was hoping the brochures would give me a small taste of one field.

In 1965, the draft was not a good barometer of anything but the Infantry and a rifle. I saw it happen to several friends and was afraid it would happen to me. I had to circumvent that if I could.

After supper, I sat down with mom and dad to discuss my options. The lack of family funds ruled out college, so enlistment was my future. Collectively, with some influence from dad's long-standing commitment to the National Guard, I chose the United States Army.

I had no problems sleeping on my decision, and in the morning, Mom drove me to the recruiting office in Pawtucket. It was a bitterly cold morning, and Mom's car had difficulty cranking over, but we eventually made our way there. We climbed an old ball and claw staircase to the second floor. Suddenly, I was catapulted back into a black and white movie at the turn of the century. There were heavy wooden doors with half-frosted glass and half wood-panel; An enlistment poster of Uncle Sam, pointing his finger at me, covering a portion of that glass. The dark oak of the door complimented the fainted dirty yellow paint on the hallway walls. It all looked very old and foreboding, fearful, and too familiar.

Opening the door for mom, we walked into a bright, modern-looking office with a polished oak desk, waxed tiled floors, padded folding chairs, and fluorescent lighting. Recruiting posters, unit insignias, and crests covered the walls. Behind the desk stood a man of pure inspiration, cut to the most refined form, wearing a freshly pressed sergeant's uniform with golden chevrons, three up and three down, on his sleeve; imposing; impressive. I introduced myself, and my mother then sat down and started asking what my options were for enlistment into the Army.

He went into a well-scripted dissertation of everything the Army has to offer. I answered his endless list of questions directly.

"Yes, I know there's a war on. No, I have no plans for college. I can't afford it anyway."

He had questions; I had questions. I didn't think I was prepared enough to go to college. My courses in high school were trade-related, primarily electrical. The required math, English, and history only compounded the layers of study materials; all so I could stick my finger in a wall socket to tell you if the 'juice' was on or off. My older brother, Aaron, left home a year ahead of me, enlisting in the Army. The tradition in the family was military service after high school; neither of us wanted to put an end to that tradition now. I told the recruiter what I knew of dad's service time. He just smiled with approval. The recruiter saw the Army's flyer in my hand and asked me, "Did you find anything interesting in that pamphlet, son?"

I told him, "Yes. The Army Aviation program. I thought I might follow in my father's footsteps. Aviation got in my blood watching war movies on TV. I always looked for the bombers with the big "A" on the tail. Dad was proud of serving with the 8th Army Air Corp."

Mom was surprised to hear me say that. She knew Aaron and I enjoyed watching the movies with dad but didn't know I carried that much pride.

"Do you want to feel that same pride, son? You can," the Sergeant emphasized.

"We don't have the bombers anymore, but our aviation program is just as complex. Today, we're using smaller planes and helicopters. If it's bombers you want, the Air Force is two doors down the hall."

I stared at the enlistment form in front of me, then at the Sergeant. I thought of the story I might tell my children one day, that I was an airplane mechanic, just like their grandfather. I read of the different types of aircraft the Army used today and decided it would be a promising career for me.

"The field of Army Aviation is growing all the time, son. You'll be ahead of the pack when you get out. You'll see. It's a good field, a damn good field. Your aptitude tests show you are qualified to handle the job. It doesn't make sense to pass it up."

The recruiter sounded a bit desperate for me to sign, as if he was going to lose a commission on the sale if I didn't. I could see the upside of Army Aviation, and I did have the confidence, mechanically and electrically. With some excitement, I made up my mind, "That's what I want, Army Aviation."

I signed the papers, never hearing the pledge I took; "Raise your right hand and repeat after me, 'I, Robert Lemon, affirm to protect and defend the United States of America, mom, the flag, and apple pie,' etc., etc. Rows of soldiers passed through my head wearing the faces of family members, telling me not to let our family tradition go by. I thought a lot about the signing. That decision would affect the rest of my life, but I knew Dad would be proud. His concern was the war in Viet Nam and what it might do to me. Once the handshake passed across the Sergeant's desk, and the ink was dry on the enlistment form, I had the rest of the semester to think of my future and what I just did to it. Graduation was coming in six months, and I had to be ready. As soon as the principal handed me my diploma, the clock would start counting down, ten days. That's all I would have after graduation, ten days. Reaction from family and friends was mixed; some were proud, others said, "You are crazy. They're gonna send you to Viet Nam." Those that understood wished me a hearty good luck. Those I asked to write me said they would. I told them,

"I will be watching for your letters."

After ten days, I found it hard to leave. It would be my first time away from home for an extended period. My younger siblings weren't sure what I was doing, where I was going, when was I coming back? Mom and dad knew what was going on. They just sent their first-born son off a couple of months ago. Now he was safe in Germany, and there was no need to worry.

"It's only Basic Training, Ma. I'll be fine." I told her.

Mom drove me to the recruiting center early that June morning. Scattered showers were in the forecast, but mom was a good driver. We arrived at the recruiting station and went in to meet the Sergeant. He and four other young men were waiting for me so we could make the trip to Quonset Point Naval Air Station. There we would meet up with other young men and board buses to Ft. Dix, N.J. The sergeant gathered the papers he needed, and we went outside to his car. As we were getting into his car, he turned to the waiting parents,

"Your sons will be fine, folks. The Army will take good care of them. We'll make men out of them."

C H A P T E R   2

A Basic Beginning

I laughed, kissing mom on the cheek, then gave her a deep and loving hug. I told her I loved her and took a seat in the Sergeant's car. The recruiter's blue '65 Plymouth station wagon was not much to look at. It had a US Army logo on the door and government license plates. The seat behind the driver was a patched, blue fabric bench seat — five of us headed for a life-changing journey. At Quonset, busses would be waiting to take us to the US Army Training Center at Ft. Dix, N.J., the Basic training post.

Mom waved goodbye as she stood on the sidewalk, her pocketbook shielding her from the light rain, just beginning to fall. I could see the tears on her face through the watery sheen of the car's window. She tried hard to hide her emotions, as dad did before he left for work a couple of hours earlier. He managed an expected handshake and wished me luck as he left for work. I wanted more than that from him, but I didn't know what.

I waved goodbye to mom while holding back my tears. I felt unsure, now, about my enlistment but had to go through it. I wondered how dad felt when he enlisted in 1938. Times were different then. The whole of the people backed the war. The Vietnam War was heavily protested across the nation, and it was a governmental war. I think that's what scared mom and dad the most.

Dad was not a demonstrative person, cry sometimes, but not often. He would get angry and show it. He would let us know when we did something wrong. I felt the back of his hand a couple of times because I did some things stupidly, things I shouldn't have done. But this time, I think I did it right.

As we pulled away, I began to take stock of where I had been; what I had done the last 18 years; living in Pawtucket seemed so long ago.

C H A P T E R 3

Ancient Memories

"*It felt like we left Pawtucket and Benefit Street not so long ago, to Ashton Village, a tiny hole in the ground with a textile mill alongside the Blackstone River. The two-bedroom, 2nd floor flat in the city couldn't keep up with the family's growth. Mom and dad found an apartment in the country, the right half of a one-hundred-year-old, red-brick duplex with four bedrooms. It had one bathroom, a tiny kitchen; a decent-sized parlor; and a large dining room. There was even a backyard for us to play in, trees across the street for climbing. We didn't have that in the city.*

Seven other duplexes filled our side of the Village. There was a giant concrete bridge, part of the George Washington Highway, a hundred feet above the river, on the other side of the Village. There were also a few three-story duplex apartments and a couple of others like ours, rounding out the village make-up.

I'd run across Store Hill Road to the 'other side', that's what we called the other half of the village. There I'd meet up with friends, searching for an empty apartment to play in. We would sneak past tenants so we could play on the third floor. The tenants would always throw us out, telling us never to come back. That never worked.

The four-story mill made blankets for soldiers and horses during the Civil War but had stopped making cloth fabric in the mid-'50s. Then, when I turned ten, it began producing fiberglass, something brand new to everybody. That forced the construction of a second factory a mile down the track, where they made green, fiberglass marbles. That process made it easier to ship them. They were moved in large cardboard boxes holding a million marbles, or so it seemed. We could see those million marbles when the reinforcing strap around the cardboard box broke. There would be marbles forever, all over the ground. The kids in the village would gather and scoop them up, taking them home. They were fun to play with but also dangerous.

The marbles would fit perfectly in the barrel of a Daisy BB gun if we took the center rod out. One marble would shoot out and explode when it hit a hard object, like a wall or stone. You could get fiberglass pieces in your eyes if you didn't cover them. The glass shards were very sharp.

When we played war, or Cowboys and Indians, the marbles in the BB guns made it easier to hit our targets, but those marbles hurt. Some of the kids got bruises on their skin, right through their clothes, after a hit by a marble. It didn't take long before the parents heard about our 'wars' and put a stop to it. I still have some of those green glass marbles.

In 1ˢᵗ grade, Aaron and I would walk up the hill to the four-room schoolhouse. Each room had two classrooms, which made up the eight classes to complete the elementary school. The teacher wouldn't sit Aaron and me next to one another. I didn't know why, but that was okay. Our 2ⁿᵈ year proved to be eventful. Aaron went on to 2ⁿᵈ grade while the teacher held me back. Our folks were unhappy about it and asked why I couldn't advance to the next class with my brother. The teacher told my parents I was deficient in math. I told my parents I didn't lack in anything and explained my reasoning to the battle-ax teacher holding me back. I solved a math problem outside the way she taught us, and she didn't like it. Her method was supposed to be the only way.

"That's the way it is taught in the book, and that is the way you will learn it," she would say.

I did not do it that way. I looked at my problems and found a way to solve them more quickly. I understood what I was doing, finished my paper, and handed it back to my teacher. She asked me,

"How did you solve these problems so quickly, Robert?" I explained how I did it, and she promptly decided to read me the riot act of how not to solve math problems. The teacher's only reason for failing me and tearing up my paper was that I didn't do it her way. In my defense, the argument I gave her resulted in me walking down to the principal's office for the commensurate tongue-lashing and subsequent punishment of staying after school for a week. My parents were not very happy with me or the teacher, or the school. Their argument didn't go anywhere, and I was held back one year, finishing elementary school with my sister Lorry, one year behind me in age. So instead of Aaron and I being the two Lemons in each class, it was Lorry and me. But for five years in a row, there was always a Lemon in any teacher's class.

That old 4-room school building still stands but has a different function now. It has been turned into the administration building, and a new eight-class grade school was built a mile away. It is a lovely, modern school, and buses are available if we want a ride home. There were some new teachers in addition to the ones from the old school. I think the building was designed as a prelude to high school. It was a unique experience having to switch classes for different subjects. Someone thought it was easier to have the building always filled with students during the move between classes than have the teachers move.

Graduating from elementary school in 1962 moved me to a new high school a couple of miles away. I rode the bus occasionally until I could secure a ride with a friend or, eventually, use my mother's car. The bus was okay, but sometimes you had to ride until the driver got to the end of his route. That made for a long ride home. High school was different from elementary school: more classrooms, longer times between classes, more walking, and late lunches. It was a headache just trying to learn new things, never mind learning the layout of the school."

As graduation approached the impact of Basic Training suddenly interrupted my daydreaming. My ten days free time after graduation was never going to feel long enough. I wasn't going to enjoy my summer like the rest of the class. I began to wonder how tough Basic was going to be, would I make it? Where would the Army send me after Basic.

I wanted to become stronger as a person, and dad wanted me to grow stronger as a soldier and a man. That would reflect well on him and hold him up to his buddies in the National Guard. Mom wanted me to be safe, to grow up, and look nice in uniform. I didn't know what my brothers and sisters would see. Maybe I would be just one of the many soldiers they see on the TV everynight.

I didn't ask. It was enough to work hard to graduate Basic Training. I hoped my Advance Infantry Training, (AIT) would take me to school for aviation mechanics. I had to make every step, every breath, every move count. It was all in my hands and no one else. Brother Aaron got Germany after his A.I.T. I wondered what kind of luck I would have after my schooling.

C HAPTER 4

A Basic Friend

Viet Nam was beyond smoldering, and the flames of war were burning higher every day. I had no idea what part it was going to play in shaping my future. My job, now, was to concentrate on Boot Camp and do the best I could. It was going to be tough, physical training with a risk of being sent home if found 'unfit for duty.' The Army did that sort of thing if they decided you couldn't hack it. I knew it would be a lot of work that I had to keep up to measure up.

Suddenly it felt like it was going to be a long ride to Quonset Point. The ride was filled with anticipation and excitement. The recruiter pulled onto the base, saluted the guard, and followed a winding path to a hanger with four buses waiting to make the trip to Dix. There must have been 200 young men gathered and waiting to board. Their faces made me think we were all going off to summer camp. But some were smoking cigarettes, reading books, drinking Cokes with their breakfasts, and talking among themselves about the things they used to do, hoping to get back to them later.

I saw sergeants and cadre standing to one side, sizing up the men, discussing how many of us were 'going to make it back,' how many of us wouldn't. A Sergeant with lots of stripes gave us a half-

22

hearted order to line up. He read off the names of the men that were to board each bus. I got a seat on the third bus, next to the last row, next to a black man sitting in the window seat. The bus was plush, the air conditioning was perfect, and the ride, I knew, was going to be supple. I could see many of the men were going to fall asleep on the way down. The black fellow looked up at me.

"Hey, wait a minute, white boy. Where are you going?" He looked tough, intimidating. I told him,

"Well, I am supposed to be in that window seat, but since it's already taken, do you mind if I sit here?" I had never encountered a black man with such solid and possessive feelings about a bus seat. All around him were Italian, Puerto Rican, Portuguese, and French, a United Nations, we outnumbered him. I put out my hand to introduce myself,

"Bob Lemon, I come from Ashton Village, and you?" I asked. He sized me up and down like a police lineup, then said,

"Name's Robbins, Al Robbins, from Eastham." We stared at one another, briefly, when he added,

"Well? You gonna sit? We ain't goin' nowhere till you plant your ass down."

I placed my small bag under the seat and my ass in the middle seat. Al fell asleep with his head resting against the cool window.

"That didn't take long," I said to myself as I reclined my seat for the long ride to New Jersey. I started wondering if the recruiter had given me the truth about the schooling I asked for, Aviation Mechanics. Stories were going around about some recruiters lying to the men they finagled to enlist, giving them false promises of schooling and a high level of training when many men were not qualified to attend those schools. Electricity was my training in high school, and I was a fast learner with a wrench in my hand. Technically I found engines not as tricky as told to me. Understanding how planes fly was not difficult for me, so I gave myself credit for being ahead of the game, and I felt good about it. But I had to, *"Get through Basic, first, Bob. Get through Basic, first."* That crazy mantra kept going through my head.

I found the name of the Post came from some General that served in the Civil War. The Ft. Dix U.S. Army Training Center, established in 1917, was part of a joint operations consolidation between the Air Force Base and the Lakehurst, NJ Naval Station. Ft. Dix had been training, mobilizing, and demobilizing troops since WWI. The General became a US Senator and then Governor, so they tacked his name on the gate out front. I looked that up in one of dad's books.

The buses pulled up to the main gate at 1830hrs, 6:30 PM, and all the men were hungry. As soon as we got off the bus, our first meal was good old Army chili. It tasted good, and everyone enjoyed it. By 2000hrs, 8:00 PM, we had marched to the barracks of our respective companies and were told to hit the rack.

"Morning comes early, gentlemen. Be ready." I heard a voice but only caught a glimpse of a soldier in a crisply pressed uniform. There may have been a few stripes on his sleeve, but I got a better view at 0530.

CHAPTER 5

Ten-Hut Days

"All right, ladies, out of those racks. Formation in 10 minutes, and I want to see every swinging dick out here. Now hit it!" and the Sergeant left us to scramble and get ourselves out front.

"Line up on me, two lines," he barked. We were still tucking in shirts, fastening belts, and tying up boots when the next order came without warning,

"Company, a-ten-hut!" It came from the First Sergeant.

"My name is First Sergeant Ashcroft, but you slimy ball suckers will call me First Sergeant. Your company commander is Lieutenant Santos, and you will address him that way. He will speak to you this afternoon at approximately 1400hrs., and you will listen. You will pay attention, or you will answer to me."

The First Sergeant was a well-built man, about 35-years old. His job was to make men out of the boys that got off the bus 12 hours ago. He bellowed,

"Company, Left, Hace! Double time, Harch!" We followed him, and he followed us as we marched 5 miles before breakfast. Brought to attention in front of our barracks, the First Sergeant had us drop and give him 20 pushups. He was a taskmaster. Most of the men in our platoon were 18 or 19 years old, and of course, he was the 'old man,' but not one of us wanted to tangle with him. Breakfast wasn't quite so welcome; it was the same chili we had the night before.

We followed the First Sergeant and his cadre through every step and drill they led; rifle range, grenade range, obstacle course, hand to hand, everything, and they beat us all.

"What are you numbnuts going to do in combat?" they would ask us. "Throw up your hands and give up? You will surely come home in a box after the VC cut you up."

Words like that always made the second round of browbeating harder than the first. Trying to beat the sergeant at a game he knew all too well was tough, but some of us did it. Those that had a hard time got to play a second and third time until they got it right.

Everything we did right brought words of praise from the First Sergeant. They were hard words but encouraging ones. It made us all eager and stronger.

Hollis

Eager? Yes. Stronger? Yes. Able? Not all of us. There was one fellow I remember well, Hollis. He had a large, woodsman's form for a young man. I could only akin his face to a large working horse, like a Morgan. His body was thick, not fat, just thick and muscular. He said he came from God's Country, upstate Vermont. That struck me right away. I had never heard of God's Country being in upstate Vermont. Why didn't God pick Rhode Island? Here I was coming from a state, not too far from him, and had never seen a woodsman, not even on TV. I thought,

"We've got more shoreline than he has trees, but Vermont is probably not as crowded."

Here I was, marching alongside a true 'mountain man.' I was amazed. After a few moments, my surprise led to shame. "Men like this, you only read about in National Geographic." I felt stunned and embarrassed at the same time. My mother would not be happy about my assessment of this fellow from Vermont.

I never could remember his last name, but he definitely stood out. He must have gotten on the previous or maybe the end bus when we left Quonset. He stood 6'3" and probably weighed 250lbs. He was a farm boy from the get-go. His shoes were a size I had never seen before. He walked shoulders drooped, and he plodded when he walked, at one speed. He couldn't run, he could hardly march, but he was one hell of a shot on the rifle range. Yet, that wasn't enough to save him. After three weeks, the Army drummed him out as unable to cooperate. I guess you call that incorrigible. He was released to return home to Vermont, never to see graduation. The Sergeant got all over him every chance he could; he gave him KP and latrine duties more than anyone else. The First Sergeant didn't want to say it aloud, but word had gone through the company that he said something that wasn't very nice. No one likes hearing those kinds of things, but we understood what the Sergeant meant; it was better for that fellow that he go home than stick around getting abused all the time.

> ***"Jody was home when you left,***
> ***You're right,***
> ***Your momma was home when you left,***
> ***You're right..."***

Those were some of the words we sang to mark our cadence when marching. But there were other, more colorful words the sergeants used that I am not going to repeat. It was all designed to teach us our left foot from our right and how-to step-in time with the other men while marching. It had something to do with discipline and order. For me, it wasn't difficult; I saw lots of it on dad's 8mm movies.

Some men in the company could not get the hang of marching; they kept tripping over their bootlaces. Those men didn't do very well during their Basic. A few men washed out early and were either sent home or got a second chance with another company. They would start their basic training all over again, not like Hollis. Some were trouble; mouthy, pranksters, and tough guys. What a black mark on their life, I thought.

I felt sorry for them but could only concentrate on my training, and I was determined to make it all the way to graduation. The eight weeks weren't easy for me. Always on the heavy side growing up, I developed a determination to see things through. I shed a few of the 200 lbs. I carried through high school and managed to make my eight-minute mile in seven minutes, 55 seconds. The Sergeant wasn't happy with my results, but he recorded my time as acceptable. He smiled with my results on the rifle range, though.

I don't know how many men graduated from Basic or flunked out and went home in shame, but I was determined to make my father proud; no shame would follow me home. I often thought of Hollis clumsily going through the field exercises; it was funny and shameful to watch. His feet couldn't fit into the boots the rest of us wore, and when he marched, his arms, too heavy to swing in cadence. Hollis was a good shot on the rifle range and some men would tease him about his hunting skill. The kidding stopped when they saw his expert marksmanship abilities. The Sergeant commented with excitement,

"That is the kill shot we need in the Nam! You are going to make one fine killer, son."

But those skills weren't enough to keep Hollis in Basic. Men like Hollis could jeopardize the lives of the men in the unit if he couldn't keep up. The men continued to talk about him after graduation. They wondered how many rabbits would survive when Hollis got home.

Hollis stayed in my mind for a long time. I liked him. All the men in the company did. We were amazed he was allowed in the Army. I wondered what happened to the recruiter that let Hollis in. That didn't say much for good judgment. By graduation time, though, my uniform became something I was proud to wear. I knew mom and dad would be proud, too.

The breath of the Army's reach for some drafted individuals was a long one. Some of the men in my company did not know their geography. They could not recognize that Rhode Island was a state or that New England was even a part of the United States. Some men's intelligence limits were only as far as their ability to march in cadence and follow orders. Unless they had another skill, they were going into the Infantry. I was satisfied with my ability to take orders and understand the tasks given to me. My progress was steady and satisfactory. I hung on with a keen sense of patience and pride for graduation day.

The Army cut our orders for A.I.T., Advanced Infantry Training, the day before graduation. Some liked to call it Advanced Individual Training, but it meant the same thing. I wondered what happened to Al Robbins and where he was going for his A.I.T. I hadn't seen him at all in Basic, but I felt sure he was tough enough to make it. I had heard a few men say they would stick close to Base to avoid missing rides to their next duty station.

They may have feared a little too much celebrating at home would keep them from getting back on time. I had ten days to go home and relax, get reacquainted with that special girl. Special girl? Hm! Then back for the ride to my next Post, the United States Army Transportation Training Facility in Newport News, Virginia, the school for training helicopter mechanics.

"Another milestone," I thought. "That one should be more to my liking and skill level."

CHAPTER 7

Ten-Day Break

I got home as fast as I could so I could see my folks again. Mom and dad were happy my schooling would be something I could use in the outside world when my three-year hitch was over. Turning a wrench and getting my hands dirty was something I didn't mind. I could quickly get used to seeing successes each workday.

That first supper home with the family had me asking questions about some of my neighborhood friends. Where did they all go? Mom told me of a couple of funerals held in the area for soldiers killed in Viet Nam.

"One was Alex Bolan, from Mendon Road. Did you know him, Bob?"

"Yeah, I knew him. He was a nice guy; he played on the football team, wide receiver, I think. But he could be a jerk sometimes. He took chances, on and off the field, that most of the guys wouldn't take. That might have been what got him killed."

"You don't know that son. Who was the other one, Bernie?" That was Dad's pet name for my mother.

"Charles Rowe, I think. He was in the class with Arthur, wasn't he?"

"Yes," said Lory. "He went out with Virginia Hart, one of my friends. She was heartbroken when she heard. They were writing back and forth; they had plans to get together when Chuck returned home. That won't happen now."

"Did the paper say how they died?" I asked.

"I spoke to Alex's father at the funeral," Dad explained. "His father told me Alex was on patrol when his squad came across a tunnel a VC had run down into. When they went to check it out, a grenade went off, killing Alex and another soldier. The paper said a sniper killed the Rowe boy while he was on guard duty." Dad lowered his head and whispering softly, "This stupid, goddamn war!"

If you spoke of Viet Nam, you talked of combat.

Viet Nam had invaded our classrooms, too, to the point several students had found patriotism, deciding to drop out, sign up, and fight the commies. The principal of our high school, Mr. Reynolds, tried to talk them out of leaving.

He insisted. "Finish your education first, boys! Do you want to get your asses shot off before you even have a chance to grow up, to live?"

High School principal Charles W. Reynolds fought with the 1st Marines on Guadalcanal in WWII and later at the Battle of Saipan. He was awarded the Navy Cross and the Purple Heart for wounds received in action during his last battle. The story goes, he was wounded, saving the lives of his platoon caught in a crossfire, and that wasn't his first incident. After completing 12 years of service to his country and acquiring the rank of Master Gunnery Sergeant, he was medically retired from the Corps; then, he attended Brown University. His emboldened disregard for his own life while saving the lives of his buddies was how he approached life as a civilian, and as a teacher and principal. He was rough and challenging, but he was fair.

Mr. Reynolds is a great principal who thinks a lot about his students and takes great care in guiding them to their future. He was not a man accustomed to speaking softly to the boys who thought more of their muscles and then their brains.

"Think, boys. I know what combat is and how it changes a man inside. You WILL be scared shitless the first time you hear a bullet pass by

your head. You will have no place to run when those 40 mm mortars start pounding your position, and all you can do is make yourself as small as possible to try and hide from them. You can't! Then, when it is all over if you wake up, you find yourself wiping the tears away, so your buddies won't see that you've been balling. That is scared, and it will happen again."

"Then there is the really scary shit," he said with emphasis.

"When Charlie comes running at you, firing his AK-47, and on the front of that AK- is a long, sharp bayonet that he's going to run through your gut. And you'll scream with the first thrust, but you'll not have breath left when his buddies come by with their second, third, and fourth thrusts. And then you die, and the Army ships you home in a nice, shiny casket. Your mothers and fathers, brothers, and sisters, and half your classmates will stand around that casket, listening to the words of the priest or minister telling everyone how brave you were and how you gave your life for your country. Hell! You didn't give your life; Charlie took it!

"Oh, and here's the final cut; when they play taps, and maybe have a 9-gun salute. It's all so touching, too, when they fold the flag crisply, and walk so soldierly, over to your mother, and hand her that flag, saying to her,

"…from the President of the United States, and a grateful nation," or some bullshit."

Principal Reynolds would then turn and stare into the boys' eyes and tell them, "Then the party is over, bud. They get to go home, and you are left in a box."

Reynold's speech always had the boys change their minds, remaining in school.

Mom told me Billy Peters, a childhood friend from the village, had signed up and was serving with the Army in Viet Nam. I wondered how he had gotten over there so quickly. I remember Billie very well; we were the best of friends. I remember…

CHAPTER 8

High School Memory

One afternoon, a group of us were at Cotter's Drug Store, discussing what plans any of us had for the future. Everything was going fine when Billie dragged me over to one corner of the store to meet a girl.

"Bob, Bob! You've got to meet her. She's for you, believe me." Billie was excited.

"Billie," I said, "I don't have time to meet a girl. I told you I was planning on signing up. "

"Why do you want to sign up? To kill commies or get yourself killed? That's nuts!" Billie said.

"No! I don't want to kill anybody. I want an education, and the Army can give me that." I knew I was talking to a stone, but I had to try to make him understand.

"Why don't you come with me, Bill? We can serve together. The recruiter said so. You heard him when he went to the school last week."

There was a moment of deafening silence while Billie looked me straight in the face and whispered,

"I already did. "

Shock slapped me in the face. I was stunned.

"Why didn't you tell me?" I was starting to drop a tear, trying to take it all in. Billie was going off without me, his friend forever, his bike buddy. He sheepishly hung his head as he started to explain.

"My dad made me do it. Like you, Bob, he wants me to get an education; in radios, planes, tanks, something. I don't know what I'm going to do with that kind of stuff. And if I go off to Viet Nam, the odds are they will hand me a rifle and send me out to kill somebody or get myself killed doing it."

Billie, too, fought back his emotions, telling me his story.

"So that's why I didn't say anything. I'm sorry. " he crouched, turning away.

Billie is my friend, my confidant, my bike-buddy. I gathered myself together and said,

"Okay. No excuses, now. So," I paused, A we both go off and serve, and kill commies, one way or another. You hit them with a tank. I'll hit them with a wrench."

We both laughed. I poked Billie, hard, on the shoulder and demanded,

"What about this girl? "

"She'll change your mind," was all Billie said.

We walked to the end of the counter, where a couple of cuties were waiting to meet up with some guys. Billie tapped one of them on the shoulder, and before I knew it, I was standing in front of an angel. She had short, blonde hair and stood a foot shorter than me.

"Joan Barret, Bob Lemon. I think you two can take it from here. My job is done. "Billie then disappeared back into the crowd. I shot him an evil eye as he left.

"I'll get you back for this, Billie," I shouted, then turned around to see the most beautiful girl in the world, at least she was to me. She was a little short, but her skin was flawless, smooth as whipped cream. I wanted to touch her face to see if it was real. She had eyes as green as emeralds that complimented her shining blonde hair, and when she smiled, it was as natural as if we already knew each other. Her skin glowed like the morning sun. Suddenly I felt, 'I don't deserve this. Then Joan, with all the sweetness of caramel, asked,

"Get him back for what?" she asked, while holding a Ginger Ale. *A cherry was stabbed through at the bottom of the straw and she looked straight into my heart.*

I froze. My only words were,

"Oh, hi. I'm, uh, Bob, I mean, Bob Lemon, but, as Billie said, call me. Bob."

Searching for the right words at this moment, all I had was, "I've seen you in school." I could have smacked myself in the forehead with that line. I didn't know what to say about how I would get Billie back. How weak, I thought. Then it started with a trivial conversation. She asked,

"What would you like me to call you?"

Staring, the only thing that came out of my mouth was,

"Anything you like. I mean, Bob is fine. ah…"

"Let her take the conversation from here, stupid,' *I thought to myself, hoping I could regain some lost intelligence that would keep up with her.*

That blind date, as it was, went well and drifted in and out of the trivial conversation. I told Joan I had joined the Army and was leaving after graduation. She asked why and I said I had no plans and no money to attend a college. She accepted that and wished me luck. We talked about school stuff mostly. We passed each other in the halls almost every day as we changed classes. We attended football and basketball games together, when she wasn't on the court playing center on the high school team. Sometimes I would meet her at the wrestling competitions held at home. I didn't know Joan was a fan of Greco-Roman wrestling. I got to like it and enjoyed watching Joan's excitement.

One fall afternoon Joan and I got together with several friends. It was an opportunity to discuss our futures. We knew Billie was going into the Army, as was I, and Joan was going to attend URI. Thom Bennet was going to college in the Midwest, while Elizabeth Martin and Mary Hannou planned to go to Roger Williams College and find a job locally after graduation. All the time I spent with Joan wasn't enough. I asked her one night,

"Would you write to me while I am away? "I had to know just how far she and I had gotten, personally, these few months. Were we playing

around, or was it more? Shyly she paused. It took a while for her to make up her mind. I think she was teasing me. But finally, she said,

"Yes." And then she kissed me.

I expelled an enormous sigh of relief. I had someone I could call my girlfriend, and it felt good. I returned her kiss and said good night."

Dad told me other boys had enlisted early, as I did, but they didn't finish school. They joined the Marines and were already in Viet Nam. Foolish heroes, I thought. Is there such a thing? It didn't make much sense to me.

The Class of '66 was scattered all over the country, attending college, or enlisted in the service. Some of us stayed close to home and got a job, some good paying, some not. Those attending Community colleges made plans to come back home, hoping to land a career teaching in one of the local schools. They were what I called 'homebodies.' But that was all right. They had a purpose, and they were going to fulfill it. Mine was foretold, I guess, joining the Army.

I tried to catch up with Joan before my ten days were up. She was at the University of Rhode Island, URI, but I couldn't remember what she was studying. I figured the first week would keep her very busy. I did see her when she came home. Her mom and dad liked me, so I felt good about that. I didn't think I'd run into any problems seeing her.

"Hi, Joan," I said, meeting her at the door. "How are you?"

"Hi, Bob. What are you doing home?" she asked with a puzzled smile.

"I finished Basic, so the Army sent me home for ten days before shipping me down to Virginia for helicopter training."

"Are you going to learn to fly them?"

"No, just work on them."

We walked down the street, holding hands until she suggested we go for a ride. I had mom's car, so we drove to a cove at the top of Angel Hill, not far from the village. Many of our high school friends went there. It was deserted this time of day, so the silence of the moment was ours.

Staring into each other's eyes made the silence more profound than the surrounding trees and darkness. My heart was beating as I reached over to kiss her. Her embrace was welcome and inviting, but I could sense some restrictions.

"What's the matter, Joan?"

"My love for you isn't the same as it was last winter, Bob. I'll always carry it with me, but differently. Life on campus is exciting, Bob, and I want space to grow and experience it; it's new and different. As your life in the Army is new to you. I can't get tied down right now, Bob."

I didn't expect to hear that from her. It hurt deeply.

"Uhm!" I sounded! I felt like I was punched in the chest. I told her,

"I think I understand," I answered, "Of course, It would be silly for me to expect you to wait for me, especially when I'm off serving my country, putting my life on the line."

"Don't do that to me, Bob; that's old-fashioned pressure," Joan retaliated.

"Yes! Yes, it is old-fashioned, Joan, just like the love I feel for you. I thought we had something special, something 'old fashioned,' that spoke of just you and me. Foolish of me, I suppose."

Joan retreated from her upset and said softly,

"I just don't feel that way anymore. I want to grow up first, see things, do things." She looked at me pointedly. "Can't you understand?"

I looked at her, stunned, but answered firmly,

"I always thought you were the most mature and grown-up of anybody in our class, Joan. I guess..." I couldn't say the rest of the words.

"I was wrong," I said to myself, confused. '*Yes, we were both just out of high school, in a new and exciting place, but I never figured the relationship we shared; that I would have to pay the price of losing her to let her grow up. Why couldn't we grow closer together? I had no other answer. I thought, 'maybe the Army didn't help me mature enough for her, or maybe I grew up too soon.' I didn't want to see her point, but I guess she wasn't supposed to wait for me. She wasn't my 'girl back home' anymore; now, she belonged to the world and was going off to explore it. '*

There were too many things going through my mind all at once. I didn't know what to say or how to say it. Softly holding her hand, I looked deep into her eyes and said,

"Well, I guess I have to let you go, don't I? Alright. I won't hold you back, Joan. Go out there and explore. I know you'll meet somebody else, how could you not? You're smart, you're pretty, and it's gonna hurt, but…." I stopped there and turned away before I teared up.

"Come on, I'll drive you home."

She sat next to me, holding my arm. It seemed contradictory, holding somebody's heart in one hand, and then squeezing the life out of it with the other. Stopping at her door, I wanted so much to hold her and kiss her right on the street, but I caught her mother watching us. Joan reached up and gave me a peck on the lips, then said,

"Please keep in touch, Bob. Don't stop writing. And be careful," she said, then went inside.

I whispered, 'I love you,' as she closed the door, not sure she heard me. But there was a pause before the lock caught. I stared at the door, wondering if there was anything else I could have said or done, hoping she would open it again. I whispered again, 'I love you,' then got in the car and drove home. One day remained on my leave; I wanted it to go by quickly.

CHAPTER 9

A.I.T. - Advanced Infantry Training

The Transportation Training Center in Virginia lies off the James River about 5 miles north of Newport News. Helicopters on viewing pedestals and static displays represented the single rotor UH-1 Huey and the tandem-rotor CH-64 Chinook I would be training on. My first impression was one of awe. They were beautiful, even if only display models. I would be learning to take them apart and put them back together again, and I was anxious to get started.

Training began in mid-September of '66, and by the end of January of '67, I had graduated two schools in the upper percentile of the Army's finest helicopter training facilities. The only hang-ups were the hydraulic systems on the ships. Each design was an animal to itself. The Chinook is twice as big as the Huey, and the mechanical, electrical, and hydraulic systems are just different enough from one another; a man could go bald looking at them. But I made it through both schools with two diplomas, and I was ready to work on them, separately or together. All I needed was a place where I could put my training to work. The Army came through that. My next duty station was the Republic of South Viet Nam. I wasn't surprised. As a helicopter mechanic, I was best utilized where the Army sent the most helicopters, and that was South Viet Nam. The affirmation of it, saying it out loud, was the kicker. I was going to war.

Leave papers were cut for three weeks back home. I was able to catch a military hop aboard a small plane to Quonset Point, then a bus ride to Pawtucket and a connection to Woonsocket. The bus driver dropped me off at the top of Store Road leading down to the village. I enjoyed the short walk to the house. A feeling of 'home' swept over me, and I began thinking of all that had gone by the last 14 years; the time I lived in the Village. When I walked in, my younger brothers, Richard and Don, were watching TV. They were surprised to see their big brother in uniform.

"Mom," Richard called. "Bob's home," and they both gave me a big hug. Mom dropped everything to come to greet me.

"Bobby, Bobby, Bobby," She cried. There was something different about how she spoke my name. I loved to hear it.

"Hi, Mom. I'm home for a while."

"How long? Do you know where you will be going next?"

I put my bag down on the staircase and paused. She stood there expecting a different answer, I'm sure. Not wanting to look her in the eyes, I turned and told her, "I've got three weeks, then I head to Viet Nam."

Her expression went from a joyful smile to a tearful frown. I could almost hear the tears fall. She put her head on my shoulder and sighed deeply.

"Your job? What will you be doing?"

"I'll be fixing helicopters, Ma. That's what the Army sent me to school for."

"Yes. I remember, now." She turned and went back to the kitchen

"Are you hungry?" she asked, without turning to face me.

"I can wait for supper, Ma. I can't wait to see dad."

"He'll be home soon. Five o'clock, usually, unless he stops at the Tap," she said as she ducked into the kitchen.

"Ok. Is my bed still ready? You haven't given it to one of these rascals yet?" I asked.

"No. It's still yours."

"Ok, then. I'll bring my bag up and lie down for a while."

"All right. I'll tell the boys to leave you alone."

I hung my head as I climbed the 14 stairs to my bedroom. I had hurt my mother; I could feel her pain inside my chest, but I knew she understood my duty as a soldier. She had lived so many years with my dad, soldiering in the National Guard. They wrote to each other while he served in England during WWII.

My bedroom was at the head of the stairs where I shared it with Jerry, Richard, and Donald, on bunk beds. It was the only way Mom and Dad could get us all in the house. With Aaron in Germany, his bedroom was now occupied by my oldest sister Lorry.

CHAPTER 10

Personally Home

Supper was never a disappointment. It was always a full table of food, family, and conversation. Today, the small talk revolved around my Army schooling and my next duty station. The boys were feeling proud; big brother was going off to war. Cowboys and Indians weren't enough for them anymore. Now they were playing with toy soldiers and model tanks and equipment in two different colors so they could tell the good guys from the bad guys. The girls were afraid for their big brother.

Mom had a reserved strength that only the worst of the worse would make her cry. Dad's worry turned into a steely thrust of advice about "being careful when you're over there." But that was on the outside, and I could see the difference. He knew what war would do and how it changed a man. He never spoke of his time in England during the War. He told us only that he was a mechanic on B-17 and B-24 bombers. Yet, I always wondered if he did more than turn a wrench.

I never stopped questioning his duties...

"What did you see, Dad? Did you count the planes as they left on their bombing missions, like in the movies? Or did you go with them, gripping the handles on the 50 caliber machine guns, watching the bul-

lets run toward the German fighters every time you pulled the trigger. You might have stayed on the ground, waiting to see if the plane you worked on, the crew you knew that went up that day, would come back? Did you clean out the spent 50 casings from the waist guns? Did you have to wash out the blood and guts the men spilled out inside the plane or clean up the body parts they left behind? Who carried out the bodies of the dead airmen that fought and died to keep that one ship in the air? Was it you, dad?"

"You couldn't tell your two oldest sons, who were getting ready to enlist, getting ready to be sent into a war zone, maybe, what they might see. I know the movies touched a nerve with you, dad. I saw the tears fall as you witnessed the bombers fall out of the sky, in the movie footage. You recognized the names of the lost planes and their crews, didn't you, dad? You had to have known some of them.

We all watched the film clips from the war, the aftermath of it all. You must have done more than turn a wrench, dad.

You had to be there to pick up the pieces. It was your job, wasn't it? That certainly would have hit a nerve with me. It had to be something you couldn't talk about; you don't talk about, no one ever does, except with other soldier buddies who lived that same horror. What a relief it must have been to find that Aaron, your first-born son, was now in Germany."

"So, what do you tell me, your second son? We built a plastic model of a radial engine together, dad, remember? It was see-through plastic, with tiny lights that fired like the spark plugs on the real engines. You told me what that part was doing while this part was going around. It was so much fun learning what you did in the war, dad. It was the closest you ever got to telling me of "life" for you during the war. You know the drill, Dad.

"You've kept it up these last 16/17 years with National Guard duties; played with the guns, you've studied the maps. You know how to lead men; give me some advice. Deep inside, I want you to talk to me, give me a little fatherly advice based on your experiences. I guess I'll have to wait."

Supper ended quietly, and I gave mom a hand in the kitchen. We discussed a few things about my duties in Nam, insisting I write home. She then told me there were a couple of girls from my class asking for my address. I didn't expect that. My only interest was wishing that one special girl would be in the mood for a steady boyfriend. Joan said I could write, that she would write, but there would be no promises on her part. My heart wasn't ready to let her go, and I knew if I wrote, I never would. Joan was adamant that she was in college to study and not spend her time pining away for a 'soldier boy.' All I knew was that I wanted to get to know her more before someone else did.

Dad came in, "I'm taking Bob up to the Tap, Det, be back in a while."

"Ok, Don," Ma replied. "I'll be here."

We got into dad's car and drove to the Tap and Die, a local watering hole. Dad tried to buy the place once, but his friend, Homer, got to it first. Dad was a regular patron for many years. Sometimes a too-late patron, but he knew all the men that walked through the door. Dad would often relieve Homer when it came time for a vacation. I know he enjoyed serving the men as much as Homer did. The pool tables, a dartboard, short beers on draft for 50cents, and a good sandwich now and again. It was a relaxing place for the men to come and relieve their stresses from home or work.

He took his favorite seat at the bar and pointed to me to take the seat next to him on the right. I was honored to sit next my dad at the bar. I had just turned 19 and the legal drinking age in Rhode Island was 21.

"Homer? This is my son, Bob. Bob, this is Homer Balor; he owns the place."

Homer put out his hand and gave me a hefty handshake. I returned the gesture likewise. He then poured out two short beers from the tap. Homer knew I wasn't 21 but his believed, if you put on the uniform, you can drink in his bar.

"On me," he said.

"Mine, too, Homer?" dad asked in jest.

"Hell, no, Don. You always pay," he said jokingly.

They both laughed. 'Short beers' was the way dad took his beer whenever he visited the Tap. I watched him take the salt- shaker and sprinkle salt on the foam head. It had something to do with keeping the head from going over the rim of the glass, I guess. I never got used to the taste or found the truth of the salt. Homer asked the usual question of why I was still in uniform. Dad told him I liked wearing it.

"Just got home from helicopter mechanics school, got three weeks leave. I didn't take the time to change." I told him.

"Oh. So, that means your next duty station..."

"Viet Nam," I said it before he did.

Homer shook his head and wished me good luck, then went to wait on another patron.

"Three weeks home," dad said," that's more than they gave us before shipping us over. You got lucky if you had four days," he exclaimed. "Or maybe a week."

That was the first-time dad had ever said anything of his service time. I was waiting for more to come out other than showing his pride while watching the WWII films on TV. There were so many questions I wanted to ask about the war. I wanted the personal feelings he had, but never found the right time to get into it. As I have grown to now wear my uniform, I think dad feared telling me too much, about the war or his involvement. He allowed Aaron and I to see the action on televisionand that was exciting enough for us. The censors of the films would not allow the wholly graphic scenes the men truly experienced.

Dad spent one weekend every month with the National Guard and goes away for two weeks every year. He loves the Army. Being with his men brings him back to the camaraderie of his days in the Air Corps and working on bombers. But dad didn't need to be in England to turn a wrench.

As a garage mechanic before the war, I always felt that was dad's true calling. He was very good at it. The Army's diploma labeled dad an Armorer, a loader of munitions, bombs, and ammunition for the 50caliber machine guns. I often wondered of his life working on those bombers, repairing them, sending them off every day, waiting for them to return…

"…having to clean out the ships when they came back from a mission; all shot up. Blood all over the place, cleaning up body parts? How many engines were replaced, dad, because bullet holes took them out of commission? How many bombs did you load in the bays, write your name on, or write, "Hitler! Go to Hell!" Did you recognize any of those bodies you pulled from the ships? Was that last one the friend you drank with or played cards with last night? How much money did he owe you, or did you owe him? Did you count the planes as they lifted off on a mission, then wait, never to be paid back? I know you counted the planes as the returned from their missions. How many made it back, dad? Count them, again, and again. Your buddies were in those planes."

Those were questions I wanted answers to, yet I knew they were the ones I couldn't ask. Dad couldn't bring himself to tell me on his own. But that's what happens to men who come home from war. They don't want to talk about it. I could see he did not want me to ask. This was a time with my dad I did not want to spoil. He had the better idea, to bring me to the Tap with him for the kind of bonding he wanted. He gave Homer a dollar,

"Four quarters, Homer?" Homer took the buck and gave dad four quarters.

"Let's play some pool," Dad said. He took one more sip and headed for the green table.

"Your game," he said.

"Straight pool?" I answered.

"Sure. Rack 'em up."

I filled the rack and set the cue ball. Backing away, I hadn't taken my first step when dad hit the cue hard and square, balls scattering across the table. Dad smiled as he walked around the table, assessing what his next shot would be. I couldn't see what he was smiling at until he started putting the balls in the pockets, one by one.

"Played a few times, dad?"

"A couple.' He said wryly. It's relaxing, and I love to win." And he did. I barely got to sink two balls, and the game was over.

"Another round?" he asked.

"Sure. You're driving." I reached into my pocket for two quarters, but before I had my hand out of my pocket, dad had thrown two on the table.

"Let's go. Rack 'em up," He said like a sergeant.

He made the first shot. I made the second and never got another. I enjoyed watching him run the table. I applauded and told him I would buy the second round.

"No, you won't. These beers are on me. Just enjoy them." We sat at the bar and chit-chatted a bit through one round and a second. I joked it was getting late, later than I was used to. He looked at me a little cock-eyed and said,

"Alright. I think your mother would prefer I was home at a decent hour, anyway." Dad placed a dollar on the bar as a tip to the bartender. Homer said goodbye and good luck to me. I turned and said,

"Thanks, Homer. I'll see you again."

Dad threw me the keys to his car, and I drove home. He didn't say a word; he just smiled and seemed to enjoy the ride. It was a short ride to the house, not a mile. He let me go in first, where we found Mom watching one of her half-hour comedies. Dad took his seat in his recliner in the corner of the living room, by the window. He always wanted to see who was coming down the street. Now, I was back, after four months away, it was as if I never left.

I spent time getting to know my brother Jerry, a run-of-the-mill, on-his-own type of kid. He played in a garage band with several of his high school buddies. Popular tunes were their fare, and they didn't sound too bad, a little loud, though.

Reacquainting myself with my younger sisters and brothers was difficult. I didn't quite know how to go about it. They had grown a lot it seemed and gone on to live lives without their older brothers around. I was lost. Don was my father's first name, and he had to have a junior before he and mom stopped having kids. My father hoped that all his sons would serve their country in some capacity. We didn't all have to go into the Army, but it turned out we did, and he was a proud and happy peacock.

I took my time at home, reflecting on what I used to be before the Army made a man of a weakling; trained me to work on multi-million-dollar equipment, taught me to kill, and go off to war. It was time for me to escape the confines of the village and make my way after Army life. The friends I made in high school were all but gone. I knew some were off exploring the four corners of the globe. Some fell across the TV screen in protest of the war. Many stayed far away from the village, while others stayed close to home. I was told a couple of my friends, enlisting before me, had gone to Viet Nam and were killed. So few remember their names. They came home in a box with a cadre of soldiers or Marines in crisp uniforms, in honor, to salute the dead and present the American flag. It all starts with a letter,

"From the Department of Defense, United States Army. We regret to inform you..."

And ends with the presentation of the flag, and ***"On behalf of the President of the United States..."***

Some parents will have a Purple Heart to display alongside a photo of their son or daughter. The same picture they would keep on their mantel or end table for friends and neighbors to see. I wept for them all, known or unknown, because they were my brothers and sisters, in arms and uniform, with dedication and commitment. I found that more of us were serving through the draft, but still, I knew more would return, dead.

Joan, the lovely girl I dated in high school, and I were able to get together and discuss how things were going in our lives.

"Busy," she said. "My courses are long and hard, but I'm making it."

"How's campus life?" I ask.

She looked at me and paused. She knew what I was asking.

Did she have a boyfriend?

"We made no promises, Bob. You said you didn't want to tie me down, and I wasn't."

"So, you have a boyfriend."

"Yes, and no."

"Okay." I fumbled for the right words, but my emotions kept getting in the way. I felt muffled inside, like being smothered by a blanket, but I wanted to burst out and hold her and not let her go. I wondered how long I had to be gone before she would start a new life with someone else.

"I loved you once, and I love you still. No matter where you go, who you hook up with, marry, have kids. It will hurt, but I will always have you in my heart, Joan."

She wanted to say something, but I put my finger to her lips so she wouldn't.

"I don't know what Viet Nam will do to me, but I guess I'm going to have to put the things we shared away someplace. I know I won't be able to give them to anyone else."

I looked deep into her emerald-green eyes, fighting tears. I told her,

"We weren't meant to be, were we? Whatever dreams you make, I hope they come true for you."

I looked at her with love slowly fading, and while I still felt something, I turned and walked back to my car. A 'goodbye' on the street in front of the dorm would have been too much. I then under-stood why the letters stopped. I was just a friend, now, and Joan was not one to share that kind of love with more than one. I didn't try to steal a kiss.

"No last kiss?" she asked.

"That would be like pulling the knife out and watching me bleed. No, Joan. I can pay that price for love, but not for nothing."

"I deserved that, I guess," she said.

"No, you don't, I'm sorry, but I don't deal well with pain in the heart." I wished her luck and told her to be happy."

There was more to say but they wouldn't come out. I drove home with tears in my eyes.

CHAPTER 11

Bye, Mom

My three weeks ended with mom driving me to the bus station, where I had a ticket to Ft. Dix. This was my last goodbye from home. The kids said goodbye before they left for school. Dad was already up and gone to work. He gave me his best shot last night; words of advice, his bear-like hug. I could feel the palpability of his concern. But I was up early this morning and caught him leaving, trying to avoid any tears. Dad never liked showing his emotion. I didn't chase him down. Dad did what dad did because that's the way he was. I accepted it because I grew up with him that way. It wasn't going to change now.

The ride with mom was quiet. I soaked up the scenery to the bus station and glanced back at her now and again. I respected her silence, knowing how she felt inside, much the same as dad. We pulled up in front of the station, and she walked me to the bus.

"You promise me you'll be careful over there?" she asked.

"Yes, mom. I promise."

"And you will write and let us know you're okay? Even your father? He likes to get letters now and then."

"Uh-huh! I have a list of all the people I will be writing to, and you are on top. Okay?"

"Alright. You have your ticket?"

"Yeah," I said.

"Ok. Now, you get on the bus and have a safe trip." She sent me off with a kiss and a hug and watched me as I found a seat by the window. I turned to place my bag under my seat. When I looked up, she was gone. And I stopped my tears.

CHAPTER 12

Viet Nam, Here I Come

I didn't know what to expect going forward, but I knew what I was leaving behind; a great home and parents, dear friends, and one girl I will never forget. This time, there were no recruiters, just me, the bus, and who knows who else was taking the same ride. Mom had slipped me a bag lunch for the trip. It was ham and cheese, with lettuce and tomato on a Kaiser roll, a couple of chocolate chip cookies, and a can of Coke. It was simple, but I felt good that mom made it herself for me. It was more personal than a peanut butter and jelly sandwich.

I thought the trip would be a quiet ride for me until a black man got on the bus and couldn't find a seat to his liking. So, I called out to him,

"Here," I said. "There's a seat here, next to me."

Walking down the aisle, he stopped to look at me, shook his head, and took the seat.

"Why did you shake your head?"

"No reason, forget it." Then he offered his hand.

"My name is Robbins; Al Robbins, remember me? From Basic Training."

I looked at him closely.

"Yes, I remember, now. How are you? How did you fair in AIT? You remember my name, don't' you?"

"Bob, isn't it? Shit, I don't remember last names."

"Lemon, from the Village, and you come from Eastham, Mass."

"Yeah!" he exclaimed, "You're pretty good."

"AIT was grunt training, man, that and driving an APC (Armored Personnel Carrier)."

"That must have been fun," I commented.

"Yeah, it was. I don't know what it's gonna be like in Nam, but I learned something else in school. I learned how to play chess."

"No shit, I play a little. I wish I had brought my board. I left it home not thinking I wouldn't find anyone to play against."

"Well, guess what?" he says, pulling out a small, metal folding chessboard and a box of magnetic chess pieces.

"Care to play?" he asked. "White or black?" I asked.

We looked at one another and laughed. He took the black.

CHAPTER 13

Old Barracks, New Life

We didn't talk much about home. Al told me he lost his job at the Museum because he got drafted. He liked working there. We spoke of familiar places we used to frequent, between moves, and spoke of things we hoped to get back to after the war. Our games drew some attention from those immediately around us. It was a fun way to pass the time and a better way to get reacquainted with Al.

The bus driver stopped at the gate and let me and Al off. We had our orders ready to show the guard if we needed to. We caught another bus to the temporary barracks for men waiting to catch that big silver bird for Nam. I turned around to look at the guard. "Suckers." He said sucker, again. I wanted to give him the bird as I boarded, but I was afraid he might chase down the bus and order me out. He did outrank me. I gave him a fake smile and caught the last seat for a fifteen-minute ride to my barracks. Waiting for us out front, the Sergeant barked out orders to disembark and soon had us broken up into platoons. He marched us inside an old WWII relic that might have been the barracks I had for Basic. We chose our bunks and were told we would have that night off. Tomorrow we were to proceed to the training field for a series of exercises.

"The United States Army can't send men to war, so relaxed, completely out of shape. So, I am going to take that sweet time you had with Jody and drill it out of you. You will lose those extra pounds momma's good home cooking put on you. You will be lean and mean when you touch down on that Jewel of the East. Make the most of your evening, gentlemen. Roll call, 0500."

The room was suddenly filled with a collective groan. But first things first, we all dropped our gear and headed for the chow hall. Curfew and lights out were at 2200hrs, 10:00 PM. It didn't take long for the men to start snoring. I lay in my bunk, drifting down through my dreams of Joan and me.

I was suddenly awakened by the ever-popular clanging and banging of trashcans and the tap-tap-tap of a walking stick. It was 0430 hrs. when the Sergeant came through to remind us all where we were. A grumbling was growing.

"At ease," was the bark from a man with stripes on his sleeves and years in his resume`.

"I will meet every one of you ball sucking mother-humpers' outside in 15 minutes. Now, move it!"

It was a mad scramble for all to find boots and greens and look like an Army for whatever the Sergeant had in mind. Our disheveled group lined up, waiting for his next order.

"Line up in formation. Company! Ten-Hut! Right hace! Harch!"

Off we went to the mess hall. Some of us fell behind, still needing to tie our boots when the sergeant called out, "Double time, Harch!"

We followed him like hens and chicks, cadence all the way. After the long night's sleep, we were all hungry but not prepared for this double-time bullshit.

"Company, halt! Everybody! Drop and give me twenty. When you are done, hit the chow line. You have forty minutes to eat. Afterward, you will line up out here. You got that, ladies?"

"Yes, Sergeant!" we all answered in unison.

I did my 20 pushups, taking a little longer than some of the other men. I was hoping chow wasn't Army chili. It turned out to be a decent meal of real bacon, real eggs, a hearty toast, and home fries. There was even a choice of SOS if you wanted it.

"Not bad," I said, "Not bad."

I was able to get 25 minutes out of the 45 and stood outside waiting for the bark of 'Attend-hut!' when everyone was present. The Sergeant marched us out to the training field for calisthenics or field exercises. Nothing was easy. You can get soft very quickly when you're on leave. I did the best I could. The Sergeant was understanding, I think. He didn't do the screaming and hollering at any one man. We all got the same shit in our faces. It might have been because he knew we were all going to Nam.

We spent a couple of hours trying to get in shape again. It was easier for some than others. The exercises came a little too soon after breakfast. A few of the men decided to deposit their bacon and eggs on the field. I was able to hold breakfast but fell somewhere in the middle of the pack during the runs. The day was challenging but still refreshing. Many of us hadn't had that much exercise in months. AIT for many of us was soft training. The schooling, seated, was hands-on, with nothing requiring a lot of physical activity. But there weren't many of us complaining about waiting. Most of us were anxious for our orders to come through, and they did. At the end of our third day of 'retraining,' the Sergeant marched us to the mess hall for supper hour, another Army meal, and back to the barracks. He came back at 2000hrs and told us our orders had come in. We were to get our gear together for an early morning flight.

It was now 2100hrs, 9:00 PM. We had an hour to pack before curfew. Everyone hit the rack by 2200hrs, but I didn't hear the snoring I listened to the first night. There were whispers of what we might expect in the morning, pushups, a run, breakfast, at least. An eerie silence finally came over the barracks. I fell asleep in peace, no Joan lingering on my mind. I closed my eyes in time for the Sergeant to say,

"Get your sweet ass's up. Outside, 10 minutes. Let's go!"

Again, it was a major scramble for everyone to get dressed and ready to be out front on time. Ready for roll call, the Sergeant had us 'right face, march'. His cadence was quick, almost a double-time. We echoed back a response and stopped in front of the mess hall.

"You've got an hour to chow down, get your ass's clean and back in formation. Hit it."

Everyone rushed inside to get some hot breakfast before it was all gone. The pancakes were a favorite, as was the maple syrup and the jam. Some men piled up on the sausages and eggs while others made the most of the fruit and the Texas toast and coffee. The showers filled up in no time, and the time spent in them was short. In one hour, we were all lined up, outside, waiting for our next set of orders. Some of us had wet hair and others' boots were untied. It was a Friday, and the Sergeant must have been in a good mood.

"Company, Ten-Hut!" He walked along, paused, and added,

"At ease. You all know why you're here. You're all going to Viet Nam. I see pencil pushers, wrench turners, and God-given Infantrymen. There are no odds for surviving The Nam, gentlemen. You do your job, you do it well, and you will make it home. You screw up? That's between you and God. Anybody want to back down?" There was a long pause, everyone looking around to see who would step forward to cower out of the trip to Nam. We all held our position. The Sergeant looked proud.

"Good!" he shouted. Then added,

"It breaks my heart to inform you that your stay with me has been cut short. Orders have been cut; you swinging dicks will be on a plane at 1200 hrs. today. You will square away your gear, your bunks, and your barracks before you leave. Everyman will be ready, with his gear, by 1000 hrs., to the man."

At 1000hrs, on the dot, every man stood at attention, fully strack and ready to go. The sergeant began walking up and down, inspecting the troops. Every other man, or third man, there was no sequence, he would ask, "Do you think you'll like Viet Nam, soldier?"

"What's your MOS, soldier? What's the spirit of the bayonet?" he yelled out.

"Kill! Kill! Kill!" we replied as one.

He stopped and looked into the eyes of one soldier, measuring the 'guts' of the man. "You better be ready, soldier."

"Look around, gentlemen. Look at the man in front of you, the man behind you, and the man down the line. You may never see that face again. That's what Nam will do to you. It'll mess you up, break that bond you made with your buddy. Unless you watch out for each other, make sure you have each other's backs, you may not make it home."

He paused, then passed the roster to another Sergeant who would be taking us to the airfield. At 1200hrs, three buses pulled up to take us to a bright, shiny, stretched DC-8, prepped for takeoff, at McGuire Air Force Base. It was a short ride filled with quiet, each man wondering what Viet Nam might be like. As soon as the bus stopped at the terminal, light conversation began. We grabbed our gear and lined up for the march to the plane.

CHAPTER 14

1ˢᵗ Trip Over

Three stewardesses and a steward greeted us as we made our way aboard. We took seats anywhere on the plane. I took a window seat ahead of the wing and watched the crew outside load our gear into the cargo hold. One stewardess was a stunning blonde in a pretty, blue and white uniform with a short skirt. Men whistled and catcalled with every pass she made up and down the aisle. A couple of men tried to get fresh but were quickly rebuffed by the steward,

"Easy soldier. She stays with the plane; you're getting off. If you want anything, just push that button over your head."

A little noise from the crowd, and he sank into his seat. He was polite for the remainder of the trip. This was going to be my first trip on a mighty jet and quite obviously my longest. I heard the steward say that the total flight time was near 19 hours. I turned my face to the window and fell asleep. By lunchtime, a stewardess poked my shoulder, waking me. She asked if I wanted a meal, a sandwich, or anything else.

"What's on the meal?" I asked.

"Roast Turkey sandwich," she replied through those pearly whites.

"This looks good," I told her. "Did you make this yourself?"

"Yes," she countered. "Just this morning, before we took off."

I blushed and stilled with embarrassment. The guy seated next to me turned and said,

"Shithead!"

"Yeah." I agreed and began enjoying my sandwich. It even came with cranberry sauce.

"Wow," I enjoyed that. Then I stopped to think.

"How many more of these meals am I going to get?"

I hoped there would at least be one more, on my way back home.

Never having flown across the country before, I was amazed at how beautiful our country is. The green grasses and meadows of the east intertwined with so many rivers. The mid-west was all pastureland and huge farms and gardens brimming with food stocks to feed the nation and peoples worldwide. The Grand Canyon was so brokenly beautiful and so long. The Rockies came upon us slowly, then burst into their towering majesty, snowcapped and ragged. I wondered if I could see Donner Pass, where a wagon train of settlers heading West never made it over the mountain and had to resort to cannibalism to survive the winter. I read where a few made it to the other side.

The breadth of the Pacific Ocean was yet to come into my window as we prepared to land in Oakland, outside of San Francisco. A decent meal, a little sleep, and some sightseeing made the trip across the country quite bearable. But that was only one leg of the trip. This big bird would stop two more times for resupply and refuel. And the trip was made that much longer.

A stop in Oakland added more bodies to the manifest, a few more sandwiches, and Cokes in the galley. The crew was used to these long hops around the world. But we men, going off to war to fight a people we don't know or only saw in the news, were getting restless. The selection of in-flight movies was small and not appealing to everyone. I heard one man asking one stewardess if she had a deck of cards. That would be a sure way to keep a plane full of G.I.'s busy for a while, give them a deck of cards. Someone else brought out a pair of dice, and the games began. One side of the plane had a rousing poker game going with their hard-earned pay on the line. The other side created a panic when a roll of the dice wound up three rows back or forward under someone's seat.

The stewardesses wanted to break it up, but the captain allowed it to continue, "Let it go, Jan. Let them have their fun. Some of these boys will never see home again. Some will come home in a box; some will live out the rest of their lives in wheelchairs. Let 'em play."

There was no sleep in all the hubbub of the games. The hop to Honolulu filled my window with nothing more than water. I grabbed a magazine from the seatback in front of me and started reading the White House's failure to keep us safe. The politics of the war was one thing I tried to avoid in any conversation on Viet Nam, whether at home, on base, or the plane. I put the magazine back and turned toward the window again. We landed in Honolulu, wondering if we would be allowed off the aircraft to at least stretch our legs. The answer was no. I think the Army was afraid some of us might run off, especially since we were in Hawaii.

I did notice the MP's not far from us. We waited, in turn, to use the toilet while some of us decided to get to know some of the crew a little better. One of the stewardesses liked to flirt with some of the GIs. They sat in the rear of the plane talking and getting familiar. There was an exchange of notes and addresses, phone numbers, and the hopes of 'seeing you on the way back,' kind of promise. I laughed as I went back to my seat.

I found it fascinating watching the choreography of luggage trucks and supply wagons, fuel trucks, and personnel making their way alongside and behind the plane. In moments, the door would close, and we would be air-born again. We pulled back from the terminal, then up, up, and away. I sat back and watched Hawaii fall away, with the islands disappearing in the cloud cover above 30,000 ft. Was it nap time again?

The stewardess did the seatbelt routine, then came around and offered drinks. The smoking sign was lit; the pilot came on the speaker to tell us our next stop was Wake Island, a refueling stop. We had another long trip ahead of us. It was nap time again, and this time hunger wasn't around.

The picture, out the window, when I awoke, didn't change from when we left Honolulu; lots of ocean with few islands. I decided to play a guessing game and wondered which island would be our next stop. It didn't take long to find out. The brakes and reverse thrusters came on quickly, so the runway had to be a short one. Wake Island was our last stop for fuel and our last long haul before Nam. The lunch meal wasn't anything to brag about. I think the airline was emptying their supplies on this last leg. They would be getting fresh supplies for the soldiers going home. I heard from one soldier that the meal on the way home was a real good one.

"Almost as good as home cooking," one soldier bragged. He found out on his first trip home. He was now making his second trip to Nam. I took his word on the quality of the food on the way home. After all, after a year in Nam, almost any food would taste better than Army food. I thought. I felt sure the meal on the way home would be better than what most of the men had gotten in the field.

Many of the men managed to get some sleep on this leg. Window shades were pulled down, and pillows made them more comfortable. A few men plugged in headphones to listen to music or watch the in-flight movie. A couple of them had books to read or were writing letters home. I just gazed out the window, wondering what I might see on this side of the world. Not much, just lots of blue water.

The landing into Ton Son Nhut was an experience I will never forget. The pilot put the plane into a corkscrew dive that had us on the ground in less than a minute. Once on the ground, the ordinary deplaning procedure went into a whirlwind. The stewardesses were up, the door was open, and we were ordered to,

"Get out of here, boys, and find shelter as fast as you can. The runway is being mortared. Go, Go, Go," she called out. It was assholes and elbows of 300 men scrambling to get away from the plane and find cover from that point on.

"Where do we go," I yelled. "Where do I go?"

I headed for an open hangar and hugged the strongest-looking structure I could find. I felt the rumble of mortars exploding within 100 yards of the runway. I prayed they wouldn't come any closer. About 10 minutes later, a quiet fell over the base and then the lovely sound of the 'All Clear' siren. It was over, safe to come out of hiding. The next boom was a company sergeant ordering the 300 men from the plane to line up.

"Now what?" I thought. We were marched to a line of duce and a half's (2 ½ ton truck) and ordered to board. In convoy style, we drove to the other side of the base where the 11th Armored Cavalry was staged. They would be our hosts for the next three weeks while we awaited orders to our permanent duty station. The ride was short, just around the base, where I saw many tanks and armored equipment.

"O-oh," I said to myself, "Tanks."

I was beginning to feel a little more secure about my next 365 days in Country. Dismounting, we lined up in the heat of this far away land and waited for someone to come out and tell us where we were going to melt. Viet Nam was hot, hotter than any other place I had ever been. I wanted to strip my clothes off and find the nearest garden hose.

A sergeant with a cavalry hat and patch with crossed sabers on it came to us and had us march up a road, peeling us off, bit by bit, to this tent and that. The tents weren't much different from the old movies on TV; there's that billowing canvas again. Only, this time there were wood supports, not ropes. The dust was the same as all the old movies, billowing in clouds, engulfing the tent and all around it.

I was ordered to the third tent in the first row of hundreds. It looked like that anyway; there were too many to count. Three men were already there, lazing in the heat. They stopped to watch me as I walked in. One pointed to a cot in the corner of the tent. I guessed it was mine. I walked over and placed my duffle on the bed.

"Hello," I said. "I'm Bob Lemon."

No reply from anyone. I felt a little out of place, not welcomed.

"Am I in the wrong tent?" I asked.

"There is no wrong tent in Nam, soldier. You're only here to wait for orders, like the rest of us; then you're gone. Say as little as possible, and you'll be fine."

I took a breath in the dust-filled atmosphere and answered, "Okay."

It was hotter in the tent than out, except standing in the blazing sun. I guessed it was about 100 degrees. There was no way to stop sweating. I walked up the path between the tents and saw a company of soldiers coming my way. There were smiles on their faces. They must be going home; their year in the Nam is over. They had served their country and were now going back to the land of the Big PX, the World; where white-skinned, round-eyed girls live. I recognized one soldier. It was a neighbor from my hometown; he lived across the street from me. We went to the same high school, the same elementary school together. It was Jack Dollen. I waved,

"Hey, Jack!"

Jack saw me and said, "Hey, Bob Lemon. Fancy meeting you here. Just get in, ha-ha! I'm going home. I'll tell your folks I saw you." Then he laughed all the more. Jack was that way. I didn't think he liked me, but he was going home. His time was up. I wondered, briefly, whether he signed up and volunteered or was drafted? A judge, too, could have given him a choice.

"You go to jail, or you go in the Army."

That happened a few times in our town. Troublemakers exist everywhere, and Jack was one of them. Maybe he made the right choice and decided to save himself from prison bars. Jack might have also saved himself from a bad police record. I didn't know, but now he was going home.

Nights were scary for a brief period. Mortars rained in on the base every day, and every day I used my Rosary to give me the strength to hang on. I will admit I was scared. They say, "once the bullet leaves the barrel, you can't take it back." It was that way with mortars, too, and they could land anywhere. One man in my tent was trying to act tough and pretend not to be afraid. I would be crying while I said my prayers, and he would come up to me and tease me and call me a crybaby.

"Get over it, wimp. You're gonna hear that shit every day, when you wake up and when you go to bed, and those beads aren't gonna keep you from gettin' your ass blown to bits." He walked up to me and swung his hand close to my face, knocking my Rosary to the floor. I turned and hid my face so he wouldn't hit me.

"Look at him," he told the others in the tent. "He'll wet his pants before morning."

His cot was two up from me, and when he sat down, I jumped up. I went behind him and began punching him with my fists.

"You...will...not...tease...me ...any...more!" I struck a blow with each word. He wasn't any bigger than. He just had a wise mouth and tried to cover his head, saying,

"Ok, Ok! Alright already. Stop. You, new guys, are going to have a rough time getting used to this war. You better get your shit together, Troop, or you're not going to make it."

I went back to my cot and left him rubbing the blows on his head. A soldier across from me handed back my Rosary, looking somewhat surprised at what I had just done.

"See you in the morning," he said and rolled over and went to sleep.

By the time the tent quieted down, and the curfew went into place, everyone was asleep, so that's what I did. When morning came and the mortars with them, it was every man to the bunker, including the bully from the tent. We bumped into one another on the way down the hole. Staring into one another's eyes, he said,

"Sorry about last night. You got up and gave me a good one."

"I guess I deserved it, but that's the way you've gotta deal with this war. You can't wimp out." There was a firmness to his voice that told me he meant business, and I thanked him for his advice after saying I was sorry.

"Forget it. You're not the first to kick my ass, and you won't be the last. I want to get home, and I'm not going to let anybody fuck me out of that chance, not even a fresh fuckin' wimp like you."

Every man in the bunker knew what this guy was saying, but they couldn't hide their fear from anyone. We all ducked every time a mortar hit, and the closer they hit, the higher the fear factor went up. The 'pucker factor,' they called it. There are some things you learn early in a combat zone. Three weeks went by, and I made more friends than enemies. When minor skirmishes would break out among the men, the big guy of the group would always step in and tell us,

"Alright, alright. Save your fight for Charlie. You'll get a belly full before you go home."

That always seemed to quiet things down. No one knew when their next mission was going to be. Rumors had the enemy at the gates and that we would be overrun, but no one knew. Charley could make a run for the perimeter anytime, carrying an explosive pack. He might kill some of us, but often got himself killed as a sign of protest against the American invaders.

My orders to report to the 25th Infantry Division, 725th Maintenance Battalion finally arrived. A truckload of new troops would be traveling in a convoy up Highway One to the base camp. They told us it was 20 klicks up the road. I asked, "What does that mean, 20 clicks?"

"This is not the US. They use the metric system here; you know, meters, grams, stuff like that. Twenty clicks are like 16 miles or so. You'll get used to it."

I didn't know how long that soldier had been "in-country," but he was carrying a fully loaded M-16 and a 45 automatic. The new guys in the truck had M-16's but who knew how to shoot them correctly or in the right direction if anything happened? My position in the truck was on end, by the tailgate. I sat across from the only guy who looked like he could save the world and us.

It was a long 20 klicks, passing some of the most beautiful green and putrid-smelling country. In some villages along the way, I could see old men and young boys pissing in the street. Women of every age were squatting in the alleyways to relieve themselves with steams of effluent flowing in clay gutters. Strings tied between trees and buildings held the carcasses of skinned dogs and cats drying in the heat, alongside hung washed black pajama bottoms and colorful silk blouses. Little dirty-faced boys and girls would stand on the side of the road with hands raised begging you to throw chewing gum, or cigarettes, anything they could eat or use to barter. It was the kind of ride you hoped wouldn't last long, one that left you with the idea of crossing Vietnam off your vacation list.

We arrived at the sprawling 25th base camp just before lunch. The truck pulled up in front of the 725th Aviation Maintenance Battalion Head Quarters. A few tents, about a dozen, lined up to represent a clean, well-organized battalion. Their only function was to service and repair the helicopters for the Division. I didn't see many CH-47 Chinooks, but a few Huey's, B, and C models were on the pad. The company sergeant greeted us with orders to our 'hooch,' a new word for me, 'hooch, 'and a buddy to hang around with during my tour.

"Hi. I'm Paul Hicks." Paul became my 1st buddy. He gave

friendly handshake, I thought. A somewhat calloused one, too. I began to wonder what he did back home.

"Hi. I'm Bob Lemon. Good to meet you, Paul. Been here long?' I asked.

"No, just a couple of weeks. The guys that have been here for a couple of weeks get to show other new guys around. So, where are you from?" he asked.

"Rhode Island," I told him. "And you."

"Ohio, farm country. What do you do in Rhode Island?"

"Fresh out of high school. No college ambitions and no money for other ambitions. But I am good at mechanical things and understanding how they work. So, the Army sent me to Huey school, and here I am."

"Yep. Gotcha." Paul said. "These things aren't Allis-Chalmers," he added, "but they still take to a wrench."

"Come on; I'll show you around the place." Paul showed me how to get around the company area, mess hall, mailroom, latrine.

"Wow," I exclaimed. "The latrine is kind of ripe."

"Yeah. Most of the guys have complained about it, but the only way to clear the air, so to speak, is to get the guys to drink more water. I think the smell today is from last night's beer fest. You'll get used to it. It won't last that long."

"That's good. I hope my hooch is upwind." I said. Paul laughed and shook his head.

"Well, here it is. It's not the Ritz but find yourself an empty cubicle. There should be one in there. You're allowed to make it as comfortable as you like. The battalion hasn't been here long enough to have many rotations, so you have your pick. My hooch is the next one over. See you at supper."

I found a clean cubicle with a wood frame bed and two shelves. A hook on the wall and a blackout screen seemed to be the only amenities. I had to build anything else I needed to make a comfortable home away from home. Dropping my stuff on the wooden floor, I went in search of a mattress. I went to the supply Sergeant and made arrangements for him to get me one. By the time I got back to my hooch, there was a four-inch mattress, slightly used, on my bed.

"Well, it's a start. Now for some shelves and something to write on."

Someone dropped a hammer on my bed and pointed to some empty ammo boxes outside the hooch.

"There is all you'll need to make yourself comfortable."

Then added, "have fun."

He was right. All the wood I needed, and the nails, to make shelves, and a desk, was outside for anyone to take. Paul dropped by to lend a hand. I was glad he brought along a saw. In no time, I had my desk, shelves, and a small closet for hanging my clothes, all before the day was completely gone. After a bit of freshening up, we walked over to the mess hall.

The darkness of Nam must have some pretty nights, I thought. There must be some stars up there. The intrusion of the base camp lights only made it easier to get from place to place but obscured the beauty of the night sky. Any ambiance was washed away with no ability to see any stars. Movement at night, on the base camp roads, was limited. Only those officially needing to be out there, were allowed, and after curfew, only the guards. Nighttime was supposed to be the end of the day, time to relax, time to go to sleep. Despite the letter writing, the music playing, the pot-smoking, who can turn off their minds to where they are and what they are experiencing? Where do you put your fear, so it doesn't tap dance on your shoulders, walk through your hair, or make you wring your hands?

During my first month, I had received a letter from a friend back home. It was unexpected. We grew up together, played together on the school grounds. She didn't live in the village, but she did go to my church, even went to the same schools. I knew her mother and father, well. I liked them. She was a nice girl, a pretty girl, polite and friendly with all the proper manner, but I found her somewhat reserved. I think she was sheltered a bit, not as open with her language as the people who lived in the village. I did like that about her. She and I could have had something going, but the letter she sent felt very pushy and possessive, which made me feel highly uncomfortable, angry, invaded, and then she dared to end it with: "*Love, Mary Elaine.*"

I was completely inflamed. The supposition of a planned and laid-out life, she inferred, didn't exist. It was even supposed or hinted at before I left. I wrote back immediately and knew the minute I gave it to the clerk in the mail room that it was a big mistake. I wrote things to Mary Elaine I would not write or say to any man. I was so ashamed. My mother would be so ashamed. I never heard from Mary Elaine again. Retribution should have fallen on my head from her parents, her brother, and Mary herself, but nothing came. Hocks and I discussed it over chow.

"I know I was wrong in what I said, but I couldn't help myself. I felt so taken, like a puppet. I mean, how could she?"

"You're beating yourself up, Bob; it doesn't sound like you cared for her too much."

"No, quite the opposite," I insisted.

"I mean, Mary Elaine and her family are very respectable people. I just can't carry the kind of love she is looking for. At least, I don't think I can. I don't know, but look at where I am; in a war zone. I have to concentrate on staying alive, not think ahead to marriage. I think it's too late, now, anyway. She's going to read that letter and fall apart, I'm sure. And she'll blame me and hate me for the rest of her life, and rightly, for those terrible words I wrote. I just wish I could take them all back."

"Yeah. Well, it's hard over here." Paul told me. "We're in a war zone. You're right, and we might get sent home in a box by tonight. Then what? Is she going to say it was her fault?

or yours? All that shit doesn't matter. What matters is getting home and doing what we can when we get back. Concentrate on that, buddy, and see what happens."

I looked at Paul and said, "You're a pretty smart guy for a farm boy."

He smiled and said, "Some of us come off the farm ahead of others. Eat your supper."

Paul and I chummed around for a couple of months. We kept up with each other's letter writing and sharing each other's packages from home. After lunch, one afternoon, we made our way to the mailroom. Mail call had been a disappointment for both of us. We could see the mail clerk sorting more mail in the backroom.

"What can I do for you guys?" he asked.

"Neither of us got much mail today, and we were wondering if you got anything floating around now."

"Well, I just got a new sack. It came in late." He went through what he had and found a pack of letters addressed, 'Any Soldier.'

"Got nothin' personal, but here are a couple of letters that can go to any soldier in the unit. Pick one. You might get lucky," he laughed.

Paul picked a light blue letter with red and white stripes on it. "Looks patriotic, doesn't it?" he commented. I affirmed his observation with a grunt and picked one with a faint yellow tint. The handwriting was very proper, in cursive, and very easy to read.

"This one looks interesting," I said.

"You know," Paul said. "My letter looks a little too patriotic. It might be from some old soldier telling me about his war. Do you want to switch?"

I disagreed with that assessment. Mine was looking, 'elderly,' that's what I remember. So, we switched. We opened our letters on our way back to our hooch's. I was surprised when I opened mine; a photograph fell out. It was a picture of a lovely young lady in a bathing suit.

"Nice," I said to myself.

"Hey, Paul? Take a look at this!"

"You lucky shit. Want to switch back?" he laughed.

"Go away," I told him. "I think I got this one."

"What did you get, by the way? Grandma tellin' you to be careful?" I teased. Paul read a portion of his letter and looked up at me, "Grandma says to be careful."

We both had a good laugh at his good fortune.

"You know, I have to say hello, at least." He said.

"Yeah, you do," I told him. "Folks back home want to say hello and be careful. But they won't raise their hand to come over here and take our place. Just as well, I guess. See you tomorrow."

We split off and went to our hooch's. I read my new letter and enjoyed reading about someone from a different part of the country. I thought it was an interesting letter, short but sweet, they say. The handwriting was nice; her name was Amanda. It was far more comfortable to read than my scrawl. So, I penned her a short note, explaining who I was, where I come from, and what I was doing halfway around the world. I closed,

"Amanda, I enjoyed reading your letter, and I hope you write back. Take care, Robert."

I saw Paul the following day and asked how his letter writing was going with his new friend.

"It's from a middle-aged woman in Nebraska. She said she had just lost her husband in Nam. He was a foot soldier and got hit on patrol. She joined a group of other women who had lost their husbands or children in the war. Now we all write to "Any Soldier." It helps to dampen the pain of our loss."

"I don't know, Bob. It all sounds kind of depressing. I may not be writing too many letters back."

"Why don't you wait and see what she does. You just can't stop writing, especially if you told her anything about yourself."

"Yeah. I guess you're right. How are you doing with that babe you picked up?" Paul asked.

"Well, one letter won't say much. 'Hi, how are you, and stuff. I know she's 19, works for a communications company, and has a couple of brothers and sisters. They live in a bedroom community in West Virginia. I guess I'll continue writing as long as it doesn't get too heavy on politics. She's protesting the war with a bunch of friends from work or something. We'll see."

"The picture is nice, though, isn't it?"

"Yeah, it is. Hey, maybe you got lucky, and she'll be waiting for you when you get home."

"Wouldn't that be nice?" I said.

Paul and I hadn't been to breakfast yet when the company clerk came out waving me down.

"Hey, Lemon. Get your stuff together. Orders came down for a couple of Huey guys to head down to the gun-ship company. You drew the short straw."

"But I haven't had my breakfast yet," I told him.

"You can have breakfast with them. I hear they eat pretty well. Here are your orders; grab your gear. There's a jeep heading that way now; he'll give you a lift."

I looked at Paul; he stared at me with a big shit-eating grin and said, "Aren't you the lucky one. You get to play with the big boys."

I asked, "What do you mean, the big boys?"

"Those guys play with guns; -60's, and rockets, and I hear they're going to get miniguns pretty soon. Oh! The
excitement of it all."

He stuck one hand out to shake my hand and tapped me on the shoulder with the other one. "Good Luck, Bob. It's been nice knowin' ya. Come back up this way when you get a chance. If you leave anything behind, I'll get it down to ya."

We both stood in the road and looked at one another. I was dumbfounded. Then Paul said,

"You better get your shit together, jeeps waiting for you. At least you'll get a good breakfast." Then he laughed.

I walked into my hooch, stuffed all I had into my duffle; clothes, boots, loose paper, pencils, pens, and assorted food items I had managed to stockpile. Walking out, I found Paul waiting for me. I looked at him and said sincerely,

"Keep in touch, Paul. We're not through yet." I got into the jeep and waved goodbye. I turned to see him standing there with his arms crossed, shaking his head. The last time I saw Paul Hicks, he had his big farmer arms crossed his chest. Three months later, as he was rotating home, the Huey giving him a lift to Ton Son Nhut was shot down, and Paul was killed in the crash. Everything Paul and I did together suddenly disappeared.

All I could see was his face, fading, like smoke, and then, gone. I was shocked to feel that my first friend was dead, and I'd never see him again.

I made my way to the Chaplin's office to see if he could help me deal with my feelings. There was more hope than solid results at that sit-down. I walked out shaking my head, wondering why I went in. The last time I saw that Chaplin was when I went to mass in Viet Nam. He wasn't any wiser on the altar with his sermons than he was when we talked. The following Sunday morning, I took a walk to the Red Cross Station to say hello to the Donut Dollies. They were an exceptional group of women. To leave their homes and come to Viet Nam to serve coffee and donuts to the G.I.'s. They must have a second agenda besides giving away donuts. It must have been the comfort, the laughter, the escape from the horror of war. They helped ease the loneliness and the desperation some soldiers feel being away, so far away from home. I enjoyed the conversations I had with some of them. They were very nice ladies. Bless you, Donut Dollies, and your coffee and donuts.

CHAPTER 15

Old Roads, New Beginnings

The 725th pulled maintenance on a variety of helicopters. There were tiny H-13s, with the bubble front end and the four-cylinder Franklin engines, the Bell-47 Observation Helicopter, and the Hueys, in C and D models. We had a Cobra under the shed once, but it didn't stay there long. Charlie walked a few mortars up the runway one night and made short duty of that Cobra. The only flight time it had on the books was when they flew it up to the Battalion. The only Chinooks I saw were constantly flying in with a Huey sling-loaded under it. Now I was going to work on gunships and their armament. That'll be different. My jeep driver dropped me off in front of 25th Avn. BN. HQ. It looked the same as all the other HQ's on base, one big sign out front, stating who they were, decorated with the unit crest.

"Hm," I thought, "That's the mountain in Hawaii, Diamond Head. Nice."

I walked into HQ and presented my orders to the company clerk. His name was Wells, and he looked a few years older than me. His uniform was as casual as mine because the

Army tends to relax rules regarding wearing uniforms in the tropical heat. The air conditioner was no more than a 14" fan blowing at high speed. It did nothing to lower the temperature; it just blew the hot air around.

"Alright, Private Robert Lemon, welcome to the 25th Aviation. Have a seat while I finish your paperwork. You haven't been in country long, huh? How do you like Viet Nam so far?" He asked, banging away on an old Smith-Corona.

"Ah, call me Bob. It's hot," I replied.

"...and it's only morning. You'll get used to it, acclamation it's called; takes about a month or so."

"Then why haven't I gotten used to it yet? I've only been in-country since March."

The clerk just smiled and shrugged his shoulders.

"Okay, paperwork's all set. I'll show you to your hooch."

Walking back outside was a blast to the face in the relentless heat.

"Acclamation," I thought. "I've been here for almost four months, and I still haven't gotten used to it."

"Here you go. You'll find an empty cubicle on the left as you walk in. Somebody will give you a hand fixing it up. Good luck."

"Oh," he said. "Chow hall is down the end of this road; turn left. Or you can follow other men going there. You have about 90 minutes before they close the hall. Cookie is a prompt man; you don't want to piss him off if you like to eat."

I made the most of the short time I had before breakfast. Chow time was calling me to the mess hall. I left my things on the hard, wooden bed and headed across the compound to the mess hall. I arrived in time for a lineup of hungry troops. Pilots and officers first, if they were up on time. It wasn't a bad menu either. Of course, there's not much to choose from. You stand in line, and they dump it on your tray. It's all good but different from the 725th. I could tell neither outfit used the same cook. The smells here were more nose friendly. There's something special about real bacon and eggs that just smells right. It tells you there's going to be something outstanding on the menu. I was right more often than not, but sometimes the surprise of powdered eggs made for a less than an energetic morning. It was the S.O.S. I was waiting for.

Willie More was sitting at a bench in the corner of the mess hall. Most of the tables were full, so I walked over and asked if I could join him.

"Sure. Have a seat," he insisted. "Got to have my morning coffee before conversation. Save it for a few more minutes."

"But it's 7:00," I said to him. He looked up at me with one eye open, so I held my tongue. I had an entire tray of bacon/sausage, eggs, and some SOS; there was even some dry toast.

"What did they do? Toast this last night?" More commented.

"That's why I got the SOS. I can soak my toast in it." I added.

"Good morning," I said, introducing myself. Bob Lemon." I put out my hand.

"Too much gravy for me," Willie said. "I like my bacon and eggs in the morning and grab a banana on the way out."

"Willie," He replied, offering his hand.

"Where are you from," I asked.

"Arizona, and I want to go home. It gets hot there, too, but the people are more friendly. There's plenty of water and air conditioning. The humidity here really sucks today. And you? Where are you from?"

"Rhode Island," I told him proudly. Willie looked at me and stared for a moment.

"They grow big guys like you in a small state like that? Amazing," he said.

"Well, I'm glad you know where it is," I said. "I've met too many guys that said they didn't know New England was part of the United States. They think I'm a foreigner or something.'

"No, I know. I studied geography in school, did well in it, too. I don't know if I can recite all the states now."

"I would have to think about that one, myself," I told him. Our chit-chat couldn't go on long enough. I thought we were having a good time. I felt like talking to him all day, but Cookie threw us out and told us to go to work.

"Hey, Will; meet me in the EM club tonight?" He looked at me for a moment, then said, "Sure."

I met a new friend and felt good about it and a little better about being in Country. Only 323 days to go. I met Top (Company 1st Sergeant) in front of HQ.

"Follow me, young man." He curled his finger in a 'follow me' gesture and led me to a construction site where a new hooch was going up.

"There's not much work on the flight line today. Work with Williams here. He's got some extracurricular work to catch up on, don't you, Williams?"

Williams turned and answered, "Yes, Sergeant."

"I want to see progress on this hooch today, Corporal. We've got new troops arriving any day, and I want this hooch ready. Got that, mister? Lemon, here, is gonna give you a hand!"

"He just arrived from the 725th. Somebody figured if he can turn a wrench, he can swing a hammer."

"Show me some progress. I'll be back later." The sergeant turned and went back to his air-conditioned office.

"All right," Williams said, turning to his crew of men. "Let's get some of these walls up."

It was a jump-right-in situation. I guessed introductions would come later. It was a new hooch going to be built in the style of a house back home, regular walls and a regular roof. There would be no canvas involved. I never figured out where the 2x4's came from. Possibly from local trees, but that didn't ring true with the geography. I saw no pine or hardwood anywhere, only bamboo. I could be wrong; the Army could have brought in a load of cut lumber from the states. Practically every other supply problem was solved that way; hammers, nails, toilet paper, TV's, office chairs, everything stamped 'Made in the USA.'

In the 100-degree heat, water had to be drunk every five minutes, but we still got the walls up and straight. When the sergeant came by, four walls were waiting for roof rafters just before noon chow.

"Outstanding, Corporal," exclaimed Top. "Who taught you how to do such fine work?"

"Private Leon, Sarge. He had carpentry experience back in the states."

"Well. That must have been overlooked when I reviewed the file. That kind of work needs some encouragement. I'll see what I can do. Head to chow. We'll throw the roof on this afternoon. Good work."

The sergeant left for the chow hall or the latrine; they were both in the same direction. I looked at Leon,

"Carpentry experience?" I asked. "Call me Bob." We were the same age, fresh out of high school.

"Yeah? I took carpentry in school, four years of it. I should know how to put up a house by now."

"I took electricity in high school, four years, too. So, what did the Army teach you?"

"Not much," he said. "You can call me Lee."

We all laughed. The corporal reminded us we had a hooch to build. That cut the laughter short. Leon was an aircraft mechanic, the same as me. He could work on Huey's or Chinooks, whichever came first. I was hoping to see him on the flight line when the hooch was finished. After the hooch's, there came the mandatory building of walkways. Made from the empty ammo boxes that dotted the encampment, it was essential to lay them down properly cause when the rainy season hit, and no one would want to fall off them. The walks were 4 to 6 inches high, enough to keep the weight of any man out of the sticky red clay. We put down a walkway from HQ to the mess hall, the outhouse, the latrine, supply, and in between all the hooch's. All the walks led to a common area pass HQ, out of the Battalion to the flight-line. It was all done in two weeks, so we were ready for the rainy season when it came.

Several Vietnamese women were working on the base. In our battalion, they were hired to clean up the hooch's, sweep the floors, make the beds (just to straighten up the room), and if you Could trust them, do your laundry. It cost a few pi (pea) to get your uniforms laundered and pressed once a week. I took advantage of the offer and found they did a good job. My uniforms came back well pressed with just a touch of starch. We all had enough uniforms to go a whole week while waiting for laundry. Some of us even stored extras, just in case a problem arose, and the uniforms didn't come back on time.

Not all the Vietnamese could be trusted, not even the young ones. Children made great spies because of their supposed innocence, but they are also well-trained warriors, carrying grenades to the troops disguised as gifts. The parents often hired to work as laborers on camp projects could be seen surveying the camp for helicopter emplacements, ammo dump locations, all centered around where they were working. They would pace off how far they were from a certain point on base and then, by eye, making estimates and drawing maps of where important targets were located.

One day an ARVN soldier (Army of the Republic of Viet Nam) was guarding several laborers digging a new trench. He watched one civilian write something down on a piece of paper then put it in her pocket. She continued recording things when the soldier approached her demanding to see what was on the form. He throttled her and demeaned her profusely as a spy, then he pulled out his 45 and shot her in the head.

He gave the paper to an American officer. He found she had written down precise locations of the helicopter revetments, the infantry encampments, the base maintenance hangar at the end of the runway, and even the weather station. Division HQ made a slight change in policy after that incident and screened their civilian employees more carefully. But one thing the Americans could not do was screen the civilian people off base. During the day, 95% of the people were friendly enough to soldiers and were making true friends with them. Some made friends they wanted to marry and take home, and after the necessary papers were filled out, they did. Some of the men continued to enjoy the prostitutes in the village. There was one soldier who got a pass to go into the village and mingle with the civilians. Many soldiers bought souvenirs and trinkets, some of gold, and sent them home. But the prostitutes in the villages had surprises waiting for the GI's that wanted their company. It wasn't unusual for men to come back to base with a case of the clap. Every day, every week, someone was complaining they couldn't piss.

"OK," the doctor would say. "Been to the village lately, have we? Take these pills twice a day and see me in two weeks. Until then, you are restricted to base."

That continued regularly, to the point, the base commander had to cancel all passes to the village for a whole month. It didn't go over very well with the men, but it didn't take them very long to get back into the village when passes were reinstated. That was when a sweep of the village was initiated. One soldier, who had gotten a pass for his second time, was having a good time, as he told the MP's until he met this very beautiful Vietnamese girl, about 17 years old. She worked in the local whore house. He had no problem entering her. But as he exited, his penis became a raging fire of blood and loose skin. Holding his penis and screaming, he ran out into the street, calling for help. Another GI, a medic, walked over and began wrapping the wound with anything he could find. Three other GI's visiting the village helped get the man back to the base hospital.

With all the commotion in the street, an ARVN policeman ran into the whorehouse and pulled the girl out into the middle of the street. He dragged her out by the hair and shot her in the head. He yelled at the people, telling them she was a traitor aiding the VC. I never found out what happened to the soldier with the split dick, but I would bet he never went back to that whore house again. The Army fills us with warnings and educational seminars about what we can do, can't do, and shouldn't do when in-country. They understand the visceral needs of the troops and offer remedies when things happen. In my naivete, I never left the base. The warnings were enough for me to safeguard my private parts and keep them where they belonged. I never thought I missed anything by not going to the villages anyway. Some men, whom I have never met, were said to be staying in Viet Nam until a cure for that particular strain of the venereal disease was found. I don't know if they ever made it home.

Willie and I met in the mess hall one morning. We got to talk more about home.

"You said Arizona was hot, Will. How hot does it get?"

"Hot enough, you can fry an egg on the hood of a car. You never go anywhere without water. If you ever wondered why some folks wear long sleeves? Sunburn. You can burn badly in no time, so long sleeves are a big help. The clothes are light, and you get used to them."

"Temperature? How hot is hot?" I asked

"I've seen it hit 105/110, but it's not always humid. It's usually a pretty dry heat. When the humidity creeps in, the temperature feels a lot hotter. That's when it gets unbearable. Something like this place."

"And Rhode Island," he asked. "What's it's like in the smallest state in the union?"

"It can get pretty warm, and humidity usually comes with it. It has something to do with living so close to the ocean, I think. The summer temps can hit 95 though not very often. The winter temps can get to 20 below, but only when we get a Nor'easter, and they can get pretty bad. They can dump up to 3ft of snow in one storm, and sometimes it's followed by another storm and another two ft. on top of it. But I like it."

"We get snow in Arizona, and sometimes up to 4inches deep, but it doesn't last long. The wind blows most of it away. The temperature will go down to 1 or 2 below, but that won't last long either. It's okay. I like it, I guess."

We talked of school and what we did there, how many girlfriends did we have back home waiting for us. What did your father do for a living? What did your mother do, if she worked at all? How many brothers and sisters were there?

"You have how many brothers and sisters?" he asked in surprise.

"I have four brothers and four sisters. I'm the second oldest."

"Geez-us!" he exclaimed. How the hell does your mother and father manage to feed all you guys?"

"Well, mom's pretty creative, and dad has two jobs and is in the National Guard. It has only been the last few years when we haven't had to squeeze the cupboard or the refrigerator for food.

Whole milk is combined with powdered milk. Mom buys the cheap bread but can make a decent sandwich with it. She buys cold cuts for dad's lunches and our school lunches. We could buy hot lunch in school but don't always. My little brothers and sisters have a hot lunch because they are fussier than my older brother and me. My sisters never eat much because they are always watching their figures until they get home. Then they are the ones scrounging around in the fridge. We do okay. My mom has a part-time job, and that helps."

"Wow. I guess that's how they make hardy New England stock." Will commented.

"Yep!" I said proudly.

Curfew was coming up, and folks were beginning to wonder where our good-night kiss was. Charlie's 7:00 PM mortar barrage was late.

No sooner did I shut my mouth and rockets were hitting in the 25th compound. It was a scramble for the nearest bunker. Willie and I headed straight across the compound to our respective hooch. It was a risky thing to do, but we knew where things were relative to our hooch's position; we found our bunkers. Four men from my hooch jumped into the back bunker, four men into the front bunker, just in time. A rocket landed 10 ft behind the hooch. The ground shook like thunder, and sand was seeped down from the roof of the bunker. We could hear stones and debris landing on the tin roof. Johnson, one of the black men in our hooch, had to be held down. His fear caused him to want to leave the bunker and escape outside.

"Stay put, you stupid bastard. You wouldn't last 30 seconds in that shit," said Tom Knowles. Tommy was a door gunner on one of the gunships. He had seen the results of a mortar hit on a building and a human body.

"Stay down, Jimmy. You're safer in here," he told the frightened 18-year-old. Johnson hugged Tommy with all he had. When it was over, Tommy told him to wipe those tears and straighten up.

"You don't want anyone to see you like this, do ya?"

"No," he said shamefully. "No, I don't."

Tommy looked Jimmy square in the face and told him, "Don't worry about that shame shit. We've all been there. Count on it."

No one said a word. I just made sure I took the lesson to heart and remembered it. Tommy was a leader in our hooch and held everyone up to the same standard and the same level of love and respect. The siren went off to mark all clear. Shortly the lights went out, and the curfew went into effect. I slept pretty well afterward.

The following day, a friend told me the 725th got hit during the rocket attack last night. One man was killed when a rocket went through the roof of the bunker he jumped into. Three other men in the company were also killed. I had a hard time keeping my shit together that night. I then began to understand the possibility of getting killed. It was 0700 AM, Charlie's wake-up call, but this morning he was hitting all over the runway. The damage was light, and no one cared. Breakfast was the usual, eggs, sausage, bacon (or water buffalo), and SOS, but this morning, Cookie was offering pancakes, too; what a surprise. The syrup wasn't natural maple, but we didn't care. It was a refined taste of home. The coffee was top-notch, almost to the point of me asking him for the recipe.

Willie and I snatched a couple of eggs from the mess hall. While we walked across the compound, I asked how far he could throw a stone across from us or up in the air. Then I asked,

"How far can you throw a hand grenade?"

"I don't know. We didn't have to throw them very far in Basic; I guess I could do 30 to 40 yards. You?"

"I don't know. I don't have a great arm, but..." I paused and offered, "I think I could throw this egg over the roof of that hooch."

Will studied the prospect and said, "That should be no problem. Ok, at the same time," he said, "1-2-3," and we both let go with two fresh eggs. Up they went, over the top of the hooch. We waited to hear where they might land. Suddenly, we heard a young woman cry out in Vietnamese. As we came around the corner, two young girls stood there, wiping eggs off their foreheads.

Willie and I looked at one another and said, "Nice shot," and began to laugh; I added, "Oh, look. She got hit with shell fragments."

We both cracked up. We kept the incident to ourselves and crossed over to the maintenance shed to get our work orders for the day. Every morning at breakfast, we'd smile at one another as we passed by the eggs.

Willie More fulfilled his 13 months in Nam and went home. We said goodbye, promising, with a handshake, to look each other up when we got back to the World. Writing wasn't something either of us thought to do. But I wondered if we would ever see each other again.

CHAPTER 16

Bored to Fear

The days were a mix between maintenance on the ships; servicing engines, tracking blades, or just getting one armed with ammo; 2500 rounds of 7.62 for the -60's, and whole pods of 2.75 rockets. The crew chief on any ship always insisted on an entire case of rations. A full day was never filled with maintenance. But every day was part of my countdown back to the world. There was always a new hooch going up until the battalion ran out of space, and the walkways always needed repair.

Late this afternoon, after supper, I would follow our walkway to the main road, down to the perimeter, and into a bunker position on the outer wire. It was my turn to pull guard duty, overnight guard duty. I quickly found out why this was going to be my least favorite duty in Nam.

Overnight watch on the perimeter wire was a nerve-racking experience, and I got to pull it twice. One night, I had a little black fellow with me who wasn't especially happy to be on duty with a 'white dude.' It didn't matter to me if he was white, black, orange, or blue, so long as he did his job. This little shit, maybe, stood 5 ft. and had a foul mouth. I couldn't tell him to shut up; he had a gun, and I couldn't shoot the son-of-a-bitch. I would be tried for murder. So,

I did my job of staring out into the Viet Nam inky black darkness, the scary night.

The usual procedure was for one of us to be on watch while the other got some sleep. This guy did nothing but sleep. Trying to rouse him only got me a mouth full of warning and condemnation. After a few attempts to get his ass up, I decided to let him be and go it alone. That was scary. After a while, I thought about calling the night watch and reporting him for not doing his job, but I didn't know how much trouble he, I, or the both of us would get into.

Good, God! Those night sounds! Real or not, I wished I had some backup. Not that I needed it. Nothing happened, thankfully, but the fear goes through your mind first. Then, like your first taste of whiskey, it filters down through your whole body, and you say to yourself, "I don't need this shit tonight." Then all your senses go to work, all at the same time.

One night, I thought I heard something moving around out in the brush. I couldn't tell how far away it was.

"Don't worry, Bob, this perimeter is guarded by concertina wire, razor wire, booby traps, claymore mines; what's to be afraid of?" Because I'm only 18 fuckin' years old, that's why, and my 'buddy,' whom I should have kicked in the ass, was asleep.

"Is that a dog?" I thought, suddenly.

"No, dummy. There aren't any dogs in Nam. The people ate them all." I answered myself quietly. I couldn't afford to make any noise. I was afraid of falling in the bunker because this kid has damn big feet, and they were in the way.

"I was amazed at how big this guy's feet were."

"What was that?" I jumped.

I stopped thinking to listen. "Shush." I thought, "Who am I going to shush to?" I turned, "Over there?"

I turned to my right to stare deeply into the night. God, it's black out here." The staring was hurting my eyes.

"What was that?"

I turned to my left, my fear ramping up as I was beginning to hear things. I couldn't pinpoint anything because I didn't know which way to turn. Over here? Over there? Was it an animal? Was it the enemy sneaking up to get into the base? I heard they overrun bases that way, and I was in the way. God, all I've got is my M-16 and a radio. What the fuck good was I going to be, alone? I didn't even think of waking my 'buddy.' So I got on the radio… "C.Q.? Sir, I can hear something moving across my area," I told him.

"Is there anything visible? Can you see anything, a light, anything?"

"No, sir," I told him.

Then I thought, 'How can I see anything? It's pitch black out there.'

"Just wait a few minutes. If you still hear it, lob an M-79 round in the direction of the sound. Then get back to me."

"Yes, sir." So, I waited and waited, not knowing how long the watch commander wanted me to wait. I thought if I waited too long, he might call me back. He didn't. Another 20 minutes went by, and I still heard the noises; I grabbed the M-79 grenade launcher and sent a round out about 50 yards. Like a propelled hand grenade, the round makes a "poomp" sound when it leaves the 14" barrel. Then you hear the explosion. It's a combination, crash and a boom, difficult to describe. H.E. (High Explosive) rounds get a little louder. And Willie Peet (White Phosphorous) makes a wondrous, but deadly, fourth of July kind of explosion, sending out burning embers that can penetrate metal.

There was only the sound of the grenade going off. I thought I heard a dog before the explosion. There was no dog afterward. I wondered if one of our patrols was out there. They do go out at all times of the day to look for Charlie, making sure he's not in the area. Gee, I hope I didn't kill any of our guys.

It was a long, damn night, and my little ass-hole buddy never woke up. Not until cracks of sunlight made their way across the camp did my nerves start to unwind. I've heard talk of a 'pucker factor," when your fears get so ramped up, your anis closes, nice and tight. I think I met my pucker factor this night. I was warned to watch my silhouette when the camp lights came on at night. Charlie could pick you off, but nothing was said about the daytime. Still, I hid myself against the sun hitting me in the back, creating a silhouette. Then I sat and waited for our relief to come. My night was about to end. I could go back to my hooch and get some sleep. The thought ran through my mind to report the little shit, but it was easier to forget him and head for my bed. I hated guard duty.

I had a second opportunity not long after. I wondered what I had done to deserve such an honor. It, too, was no fun. I was alone. The soldier that was supposed to watch with me called in sick, and there was no replacement. I hated that night, too. I heard the same sounds, felt the same fear, the same 'pucker factor. I fired the same weapon.

Then, for the first time in my life, I heard the resounding report of a 50-caliber machine gun. I knew there was a tower behind me, but I never looked up to see who or what was in it. I didn't know anyone was in there watching with me. Maybe he saw something. Perhaps he heard what I heard. When he let go with that 50, I nearly shit my pants. It caught me entirely by surprise. The perimeter lights went on, the 50cal. let go, and I ducked — my mistake. I was supposed to be ready for anyone coming across the wire. I wasn't. I didn't want to be. I wanted to go home. I hated guard duty.

That morning sun was a more than welcome sight. I saw nothing, looking for signs of something dead, wounded, or just torn apart from the 50. I didn't care anymore, not about the heat, the dust, my dry throat, or the walk back to my hooch. My night was over, and I was tired. Give me a wrench or a hammer. You can keep my -16 and the fuckin' bunker. I was looking forward to working on helicopters again.

Chapter 17

An Oriental Introduction

The days didn't change much after Willie went home. I didn't latch on to anyone else; I just hung around with whoever was there. The EM Club was always safe and full of friendly noise. Acts brought in by somebody; I didn't know who was both musical and funny. Mostly Korean musical groups with some pretty girls in the mix, singing American songs of the day. They wanted us to feel at home, but that didn't work. The song, I Want to Go Home in a Korean lilt just wasn't the same. Oh, they had the rhythms down, and the music wasn't bad, but the real entertainment value was bogus.

Now, the dancing troops that made it to the floor were a different story. One night, a dancing troop from some island came in to entertain us with their bouncing navels. They were beautiful ladies with the most curves I had ever seen. They had the 'rings on their fingers and bells on their toes, as well as castanets and frills hanging from every part of their bodies. One gal, in a purple outfit, what there was of it, got so rhythmic in dance she almost hypnotized me. The little strings hanging on her nipples went around and around. She came so close to me; I had to back up for fear of getting poked in the eye. I fell backward off my seat, knocking over a table of drinks.

Fortunately, there was no beer on my table, only Pepsi. Can you get drunk on soda? I never found the answer or the cure for the hangover the following day. But, man, do I remember that dancing girl.

Action in Nam was beginning to heat up toward the end of summer, and men were looking to get out of the country for a while. There were vacation programs soldiers could take advantage of, the Rest and Relaxation program, or R & R. It was a way for the Army to give guys a break from the everyday stress of Nam. There were vacations to different parts of the world. Many men went to Hawaii to meet their families or sweethearts. Others wanted to go to Australia to meet up with round-eyed, white girls. Still, others went home for a week. I opted to go to Malaysia. I just picked a place I had only heard of and wanted to visit and not far from Viet Nam with much the same topography, geography, and temperature.

I took my vacation in late October '67. I found the people of Penang, Malaysia, to be very friendly, but that might have been because they liked the color of American money, and soldiers and Sailors on vacation carry a lot of money. I came across one little guy, San, anxious as hell to take me around the island.

"Mister. Hey, Mister. Do you need a guide? I'm a good guide, the best on the island. I take you everywhere, anywhere you want to go. Even get you a girl, a nice girl, cheap." He wasn't a sleeve tugger, but he sure *was an ear-bender. After a few minutes, I was on the back of his motorcycle, and we were going anywhere. I let him be the guide. There was a part of the city Americans were not allowed to enter. It was rife with drugs and deals gone bad. They told me about it at the base and said, too, several G.I.'s had gotten killed there. So, we avoided that part of town.*

San was a real hot rod on that cycle. He took me everywhere in short order. He found a decent hotel for me with nice sheets, a great pillow, and a pretty good restaurant. Penang was a pretty place. The usual party lights were strung out all over, and ornamental dolls and dragons were everywhere. San came by my room one night and asked me if I wanted company.

"Sure," I said. He came back in 5 minutes and brought me a beautiful girl, exquisitely dressed. I thought he was going to be my company

and come back with playing cards or something. "What's this? Who is she?" She was a beautiful girl.

"She is for you tonight. You like her?"

I was stunned, without words. This was the first time I was ever presented with a girl who would spend the night with me. I knew what San was saying, but I didn't quite know how to take it. I was a virgin, a Cherry Boy; I had never been with a girl or a woman. Trying to be a gentleman, not able to step out of my naivete, I balked. "Oh!" I stammered, "Ok," and I welcomed her in. Then San hands me a bottle of champagne and says,

"Goodnight. See you in da morning."

"Yeah. Goodnight, San. See you tomorrow."

She was beautiful, she was young, about my age, 18. We sat on the edge of the bed while I struggled to get the champagne bottle opened. Every twist of the cork brought her closer and closer to me. I was beginning to get a little nervous. I was a virgin, after all, and this girl probably wasn't. I didn't quite know what I was doing or if winging it was the right way to go. The cork popped, and she applauded with a beautiful smile. I turned and gazed at her stunning complexion, flawless. I wanted to express my sentiment of her beauty, but my mind was lost in her eyes, so round, clear, like magnificent, dark marbles.

I stood and went to the table to get two glasses and poured us each a drink. When I turned around, she had dropped whatever she was wearing and stood there completely naked. Her body was that of a goddess, beautiful. I was lost in the moment and an erection was wanting to burst through my pants. I walked over to her, admiring her beauty, and handed her a glass. She, so gently, took a sip of the champagne, then took my hand and led me back to the bed. The rest of this dream I will leave to myself. If that night was the measure of a man, then I guess I became one.

There was only one night like that on Penang. I had to say goodbye to the pretty little girl in the morning. Though it was tempting to stay with her another day, I wanted to see other sites on the island. San and I hopped on his motorcycle in the morning and buzzed in and out of every tourist trap. He knew them all. My vacation lasted seven days. When it was over, San drove me back to the airport and thanked me profusely for the opportunity to be my guide and friend. We were friends now. I gave him a decent tip, said thank you, and boarded my plane back to Saigon. He waited for me to take my seat and saw me in the window. I waved back and watched him watch me right until the point of takeoff. I don't know what I did for him. I figured I was just another customer, and he was a guide and pimp to soldiers like me.

"Thank you, San, for helping me become a man." I then laughed at myself. It wasn't a long flight back to Nam, but I had time to sit back and take a nap."

CHAPTER 18

Back to War

On the flight back, I thought about my hitch in the Army. Speaking to several soldiers on base, I found out that if you volunteer to extend your tour in Nam, you can shorten your time in the Army by reducing the amount of time you have left on your three-year hitch. Calculating my remaining time after I leave Nam, I would have more than a year remaining on my hitch, and that would be enough for the Army to turn me around and send me back. That was one prospect I could not entertain.

When we landed, I caught a convoy back to Cu Chi. The guys were glad to see me and asked if I had a good time, did I get laid, etc., etc. I gave them an 'affirmative' thumbs up, waved, and headed for my cubicle. Everything was still in place, nothing missing, and there was a pile of mail waiting for me, mainly from Amanda. There was also a letter from Aaron and one from my dad, what a surprise. So, I got busy with the pen and started writing back. I saved Amanda for last. I wanted everything to be understood as I read her letters and for her to understand me as I wrote back. I wanted a clear head.

Dad and Aaron, pretty much, got the same letter. It was Army stuff they both understood. Telling them I was okay, feeling good, had a great time on vacation, including the girl, and it didn't take me long to write home. Writing to Amanda was a lot different. I did tell her I thought about extending my tour so that my ending time in the Army would come sooner. I told her, too, that I had gone on vacation to Penang and had a great time, even that I was with a girl. Maybe I was wrong, but our relationship in the letters was elevating, and we both agreed to be totally honest with one another. We both decided that we would wait for one another before having sex. Oops! I hoped she would understand.

I sent my letters out the next day and waited for more to arrive. Usually, there is a letter from Amanda every day, but this time I waited more than a week. The letter that came was a scalding one; she was pissed. She explained everything to me that meant all and everything to her that was supposed to be the foundation of our relationship. I had hurt her badly and wrote to say I was sorry. From then on, her letters took a different tone. I had to wait and see what would come out of my blunder.

In a previous letter, she had written about seeing a fellow from her neighborhood. I thought it odd that she would mention that, but Amanda was honest, I thought. Or was she getting even? The guy wasn't even of the same religion, and that was a stumbling block being exacerbated by his mother. Another letter mentioned an Italian fellow she had seen a few times. We had no ties to one another at the time, but it did shake the level of commitment I thought we had grown into, and she was trying to make. I let all that go as high school playtime. She was home, and I was half a world away. She had already graduated from high school but maybe not the high school hijinks. There was nothing I could do about it. So, all that put a doubt on the things we had talked about and written about.

By the end of November of '67, I had made up my mind about extending my tour six months to shorten my three-year hitch. I was called in to see the commanding officer. He asked if I was sure that's what I wanted. I told him,

"Yes, sir. I want to fly. I want to be a door gunner. It's great to work on the ships, but we've got an overflow of mechanics. There's not a lot of things left to do. The company area is squared away. There's no room left to put up another hooch, and frankly, sir, I'm bored."

The Colonel studied me for a moment, then asked, "Do you know the life expectancy of a door gunner in combat?"

"Yes, sir...everyone is saying 60 seconds."

The Colonel looked at me and said,

"The door gunner sits on the edge of his seat to get the best firing position; away from the rockets and to avoid hitting the ship, in general. That's a dangerous position to be in, soldier. I heard one crew chief call it, like 'sitting on a headstone.' I asked him why. You know what he told me?"

"No, sir," I answered.

"You don't look down to see whose name is on that stone. You're betting it's not yours'." He told me, coldly,

"I've been up there, son, and it's not pretty, but it's my job, and I know I'll have to go up there again; and you still want to fly?" he added.

"Yes, sir."

"Alright. I have your request in front of me. Sign this

form, and we'll get things going for you. In the meantime, we will send you home for 30 days, get your affairs in order, see the folks and friends, that kind of thing. Your leave will start in one week. When you get back, you can bet you will be busy. Good luck, soldier."

"Yes, sir. Thank you, sir." I left his office with a smile on my face. "I'm going to be flying."

I walked to my hooch and stared at my calendar. Marking off the days as they passed. Letters would reveal only the basics that I had extended and would be coming back. I wrote Amanda I was coming home for a month and would like to see her on my way back to Ft. Dix. I said I would be calling her to confirm some time for my visit. I knew I wasn't going to get a reply before I left. If she wrote back, the letter would only be a memento of our relationship. I posted my last letter the day I left Cu Chi. She would have to wait until I got home to hear or see me for the very first time.

CHAPTER 19

A Brief Interruption

I arrived home after Christmas, December of '67, so a big part of January was mine. The Rhode Island winter kept blowing through my summer uniform until I found some warmer cloth still hanging in the closet. I opened all the Christmas gifts the family had saved for me. We gathered in the living room to open them, and I would tell them I was going back. I expected the reactions I got.

"What do you mean you're going back?"

"Isn't your time up over there?"

"You can't go back. It's someone else's turn."

Mom and dad were silent through all the commotion. Dad got up and went out for a cigarette, even though he always smoked in the house. Mom went to the kitchen after kissing me on top of my head. I told them all the gifts were perfect, Just what I needed, no toys or trinkets, nothing to take back with me but possibly the St. Christopher medal from my grandmother and a new set of Rosary beads. But the celebration didn't last long. I found it difficult answering their questions, then thought, there were no answers I could give them.

I did the best I could to quell their fears, but the nightly news and the talk around town did nothing to suppress those fears. I had to let all that go and concentrate on relaxing for the next 30 days. I was glad there were no mortars or rockets or sergeants to listen to. I got some decent sleep for a change.

Mom was good about letting me borrow her car, so I drove down to the University to try and catch up with Joan. I got lucky and caught her after classes. "Joan!" I called out to her.

"Bob, what are you doing here? I thought you were in Viet Nam. Are you home already?"

"Well, yes and no. I'm home for 30 days, and then I have to go back."

"Go back? Why?"

The way she asked the questions made me wonder if she was starting to care again.

"I have to go back so I can take six months off my regular three-year hitch."

"How long will you be staying this time?"

"I agreed to another six months." I didn't want to tell her why I was going back and what I would be doing. I didn't want to tell anyone I was going back to fly.

"I felt you should hear it from me, not from anyone else."

"You do remember about the boy I'm seeing," she asked.

"Yes, I remember. Is he,"

"Yes. He's still around. We see each other on weekends, so we don't interrupt classes or homework. He's at U. Mass. "

"Uh-huh. Can we walk?" I asked.

"Sure." She held her books like a high school cheerleader, close to her chest, but I took it as a guarded posture, protecting her heart from me. It was difficult not telling her how much I still cared. Our best conversation was about family and any of our friends from high school. When it came time for me to leave, I ventured a kiss, and she returned it. We looked at each other and fell deeply into each other's arms.

"Oh," she said embarrassingly. "This has to stop, Bob. My caring for you will always be there, but only as a dear friend; I can't grow with you anymore, Bob. I'm sorry." She stopped, and that added all the emphasis I needed to understand. "You'll have to go now. Please be careful when you go back." She just turned and walked back to her dorm.

Disappointed? Yes, I was disappointed. The girl I took to the prom and sang Blue Velvet to; the one I held in my arms and kissed so passionately on our senior dates; the one I wanted to wait for me when I was away. She said goodbye, so matter of fact about it all. I knew where I stood. Why was I making a big thing about it? I've heard it said: love is fickle, then I knew.

There weren't many other people I could see while I was home. Most of them were working; some were away at a college, others were in Viet Nam. I heard of one friend dying in a ship collision while he was below deck, asleep in his bunk. Another, a Marine, was shot by a sniper while on guard duty. I found one friend employed by the CIA and was involved in covert, Black Ops activities. Some had joined the Army and became Green Berets, and that one graduate had gone to Canada to escape the draft. I felt proud of those that served and died, fighting on foreign soil for our government; a bit ashamed that a member of my class had defected.

I promised Amanda I would stop by to see her and meet her family. The confusion and uncertainty I felt were not strong enough for me to say no. I got slammed hard when Joan said goodbye; now, I needed Amanda to fill the gap. Joan wanted to grow up with someone new, yet we had known each other ever since elementary school. Friendship was all we had left. The differences between Joan and Amanda were still to be known. I had not met Amanda yet. She was still fresh and new. It was only through our letters that any hope of a relationship was possible.

She did leave me feeling some uncertainty, though; all up in the air about everything. She was disappointed about my trip to Penang, but she had two other guys on the string at home. If things went utterly sour, there was no way for me to know until the last minute. I felt sure she would welcome me to her home, meet her family and spend some time with her to discuss things. Maybe there was a future together, maybe not, but I had to find out. I left it that way until I could look into her eyes. With two weeks remaining on my leave, I asked mom to borrow her car to drive to West Virginia.

"Why don't you fly down, Bob? West Virginia is a long way to drive just to see someone for a couple of days. Fly down?"

Mom had a good idea, but I told her, "This isn't a business trip, Ma. I can't write off the expenses."

"We have talked about marriage, Ma, so I think I should meet her family first. Don't you?"

Mom looked at me and paused for a moment.

"Well, if you feel that strongly about her, I can't get in the way of love, but flying down makes a great deal more sense. You won't have to spend two whole days on the road. You can spend them with Amanda."

Why do moms make so much sense when you need all the reason in the world? I thought about it and tried weighing the differences, but mom was right no matter how I felt about it.

"Ok, mom. You win again. I'll call Amanda and tell her I'll be flying in, then rent a car to her place."

"Good. I think it's better that way. You won't have time to get too stressed out before you two meet."

"Thanks, ma. That's encouraging." I said, squeezing the breath out of her and kissing the top of her head.

"When are you going?"

"I'll call the airport first, then call Amanda and tell her what my plans are. Do you think I should leave early in my leave or wait till I'm ready to go back?"

"I think it all depends on how anxious you two are to meet."

"Well," I paused. "I'm anxious."

"Then tell that to Amanda and let her decide."

Moms are always full of good advice, and this time I took it. I called Amanda before I called to make my reservations. She told me to hurry down. I called the airport, arranged for the next available flight, and made arrangements for a rental car. I called Amanda back and told her I would call her again when I landed and started toward her place. All I needed were the directions to find her house. Amanda had given them to me quite succinctly. I put them in a safe place so to be sure I could find them when I landed.

Amanda had all the information she needed to be ready for my arrival. I didn't know what to expect being in West Virginia. You hear a lot about some of the people down there. Others think their comments are funny, many soldiers do, too, but I wasn't reared to think that way. Still, I had my fears about how I would find conditions with Amanda and her family. She did say they were 'kind of poor.'

What that meant, I didn't know. I only knew she was somebody's daughter. I tried to let any trepidation or fear pass and made ready to expect what I would see and accept Amanda and her family on the best terms.

I packed some nice clothes for the sake of making a decent appearance and bought a map of West Virginia. I couldn't wait to meet Amanda's parents. I thought three days would be enough time for us to make up our minds about a future together, or not.

My flight was on a Monday and took the whole day with connections. My rental car was waiting for me at the airport, but one look had me wondering if it was going to get me to Morgantown and back. It was a fifteen-year-old Chrysler; it did start the first time. It was comfortable and big, a '300'. Once on the road, I opened the map and headed for the quickest route to Amanda's place. It was less than fifty miles on the map. I felt I could make it in under two hours. I was right. With twists and turns and a couple of back roads, I arrived to find Amanda on her front porch with her mom and little brother on the two-hour mark. Her sisters were still in school. Her dad was working in town and would be home later.

The house was high on a hill in the tiny bedroom community outside of Morgantown. The house Amanda lived in wasn't much to speak of, but many of the other homes in the neighborhood were similar. Her father's misfortune at work, and her mother's inability to work, left Amanda to give over her pay to help sustain the family. It all contributed to a less than the standard way of life. I thought my family had it rough with nine children in the house, but there was little comparison to the poverty Amanda lived under. Her mom was a homemaker and didn't work. She was fair-to-middling as a cook, so eating with the family was familiar. Her dad, a true Irishman, was a lover of beer and a shot, now and then, not at home but the local veteran's meeting hall. Carl, Amanda's father, took me to meet some of his friends and bought me a drink. That experience told me to be cautious about stepping into another Veteran's Hall. I didn't need to hear war stories or get advice from drunken men who fought in 'the last war." They all tried to fill my ears with opinions and options on how to fight this war. I wasn't going to listen. I let it go in one ear and out the other. I did enjoy the dart game with her father. Like my dad, he ran the board twice and never gave me a chance.

We stayed for two drinks, and that was enough for me. I wanted the opportunity to spend time with Amanda, anyway. The house didn't offer a great deal of privacy, so we went for a drive in the car.

Amanda showed me her town and where she attended church. We passed the beverage distributor where her father worked and the school where she graduated. I was beginning to understand why she wanted to escape her town and head for a quaint little village in New England, live in a small cottage with a white picket fence. She did want to get married, and I felt it was to me. We discussed it and said we would write about it more when I got back to Nam. She was warm, she was loving, and her kisses were sweet. I hoped she would stay that way, for me, while I was gone.

Three days later, I said goodbye and was not shy about kissing her on the front porch. I felt good about our meeting, about meeting her parents, and vowed that I would take her away from all this poverty. There was nothing I could do about the rest of the family.

The kids were still growing. Her mother needed to go to work; her dad needed to stop drinking. I was glad I was going home.

There was a lot to think about on the ride back to the airport. When I arrived home, I explained to mom what I saw, the conditions they were living under, and the coal mining town she lived in. I told mom the church was lovely. Mentioning Amanda's desire to escape those conditions and West Virginia, as a whole, had my mother questioning the viability of our relationship going any further.

"Bob, you've met her only once. You can't decide on marriage based on your seeing each other for the first time. Love and marriage don't usually succeed that way. Wait until after you've returned from your next trip."

"Mom, I'll only be gone for six months," I told her.

"But things can change, even in that short period."

"Yeah," I knew mom was right. I felt Amanda's desire to escape the current living conditions at home. They were enough to make me leave. But what could change and blow the whole thing apart? Her running away with another guy, I guess. "No, that's not going to happen," I told myself.

Mom and I sat up for a while. We discussed some of the things that could go wrong and the many things that are supposed to go right.

"I know you're right, mom. You always are, but I have to leave in the morning, and you are taking me to the bus station. I have to get some sleep."

I bent down, kissed her, and told her I loved her, then said goodnight. The light stayed on a while after I went to bed. Mom worried about her children jumping into decisions that needed more time and thought. I couldn't close my eyes until I was sure mom was upstairs and in bed. Then I knew she was okay.

In the morning, we drove to the bus station. Again, mom would weep for her son going off to war. But now, she was going to do double time on the rosary and visits to church. She didn't have doubts about my returning home, only doubts about me returning safely. I kept explaining my chances were as good as any soldier over there and that I would be careful. But inside, even I couldn't be sure about that. I was going to do my job no matter what they asked of me. Dad understood that and still wiped away a tear as I left that morning. Mom handed me a brown bag lunch for the trip and smiled, looking directly into my eyes. "I love you, son. Please come back to me, to us, and be careful."

Her hug was one even I didn't want to let go of, but the bus driver insisted he had a schedule to keep. I found a window seat where I could see her wave as we drove away. "A man shouldn't do such things to his mother," I thought to myself.

CHAPTER 20

Ft. Dix Once More

I went through the same gate, so familiar, the same idiot in the Guard House and the same smirk on his face. The barracks reminded me of one I used at Basic Training. One bunk remained when I arrived, and it didn't matter where I slept. None of us were going to be there for very long. We might get some PT to keep us fresh, but it was all just a waiting game, waiting for that big silver bird to take us to war. The sergeant put us through 4 grueling days of all the PT he could think of, even some he made up. On the fourth day, he had us at attention outside.

"Men, your orders have arrived for your next duty station. You're all going to Nam. There's a plane waiting to take you there that will be leaving at 0900AM tomorrow morning. Reveille is at 0600, and every man will be ready to board the bus to the airport by 0700. Any slackers that miss that flight will be considered AWOL and subject to my hospitality until the next flight. The night is yours, gentlemen. Dismissed."

True. The night was ours, and every man was busy with letters telling mom and dad, and that sweetheart, that they were on their way. The next letter would go out after they hit Nam. Some men ventured over to the PX for what they thought they might need 'in-country'; cigarettes, bug repellant, talcum powder, more pens and paper, chewing gum. Their shopping craziness was ridiculous. They knew most of those supplies you could purchase at the PX on base. I had six months before turning around and coming home for the last time. That was all that concerned me. Sleep was less than perfect that previous night at Dix. I just wanted to get on the plane and get my next six months, my last six, completed.

Every man was up and ready by 0600. It didn't look as though many of them slept any better than I did. By 0700, we were dragging our asses toward the buses that would take us to that DC-9 for the flight over. By 0900, I heard the landing gear folding back into the wheel wells as we lifted off the runway. Stewardess announcements were just words floating by. Just about every man was buckled in and asleep before the captain's call of "...we will be reaching an altitude of 30,000 ft."

Who cared? Everyone wanted the long ride over. Only sleep was going to make it go by without anxiety. I turned to the window and placed my head on the glass. The tire squeal on the runway at Oakland, California, woke me. The stewardess ushered us off the plane when the doors opened for a brief 45-minute reawakening to civilian life. MPs were stationed around the area, securing our safety from the urge to escape the flight over or go AWOL. The tarmac was the extent of our roaming area. Cigarettes were lit, chewing gum wrappers floated about as conversations turned to each's future in Nam.

I heard men complaining about going over as grunts, having to hump the bush. They wondered if they were going to make it back alive. A few men were discussing the outfits they were going to be in and how they might be able to communicate with each other when they landed. They would be desk jockeys, so I didn't think anything was holding back their ability to talk to one another. A small group of men was huddled in one corner playing cards, laying down their last paycheck, hoping to either go broke or hit it big. They figured they could send it home and have their folks save it for them when they got back. Or as one man said,

"What the hell. If I get killed in Nam, I won't need it anyway."

Fate handed a different set of cards to each man boarding that plane, and not one of us was going to be able to bluff a hand. We all had to play it out.

CHAPTER 21

The Hell of War

March 19, 1968, I was back in the Nam. A convoy leaving Ton Son Nhut headed back to Cu Chi and the 25th, so I got a lift. I could see smoke in the distance. Charlie must have hit the ammo dump again. There was activity everywhere. The gates were locked to all civilian workers. Rumors circulated Charlie was preparing for a big push. The TET holiday was wrong for all American bases, and a second hit was expected. The Division was getting ready for it. Sappers were coming up from tunnels under the base, and "The Tunnel Rats" were busy routing them out. Going into those tunnels to find Charlie didn't guaranty you were going to make it out. The dead bodies of the enemy were left behind after blowing up the tunnels. But the American GI's bodies had to be recovered first; then the tunnels were blown.

A team, two of our gunships, was sent down to Saigon during the TET offensive to aid in the pushback of the Cong and NVA regulars assaulting the American Embassy. One door gunner was killed and one wounded. The wounded crew chief was a 26-year-old overweight sergeant that got hit in the side only because his fat wouldn't hide behind his safety plate. The door gunner killed was 19 years old, on his first mission. The helicopter banked on Jimmy's side when he got hit in the chest. As it banked to the other side, rounds came through and hit him in the back. Jimmy Younger was a friendly kid. I'm going to miss him.

Diamond Head ships were up almost every day. All units on base were either put on alert or already engaged with the enemy somewhere outside the wire. It didn't take long before I was getting my belly full of the intensity of combat.

Before my first mission, I was given training handling the M-60 machine gun, the number one offensive and defensive weapon on a Huey. It was the door gunner's favorite. Easy to care for and easy to load and reload, the M-60 was robust and accurate. The barrel on a -60 is removable, which is a nice feature when you're in a combat situation, and the barrel starts to heat up. Even in the draft of a Huey doing 90 knots in a dive, the barrels will glow bright red, telling you it's time to change the barrel. Once a barrel starts to glow, it bends to the point of disrepair, and then it's no good to anyone anymore.

I remember changing a barrel on one of the two -60s we had on the ship. Before the minigun came into play, two M-60 machine guns were hard mounted, one above the other, on an outboard gimbal. They were about 36in. out my seat and belt fed, with 7.62 ammunition. We were on an assault on a village Charlie had entered. He was letting us have it for all it was worth. We went into a dive with all four -60s going full bore when one of the barrels began glowing a bright red. We thought it was going to melt right off the gun. If it had, we would not have been able to remove it. The captain called back,

"Lemon, get out there and change that barrel. I don't want to lose that gun."

"Yes, sir." I was still new to this and could see tiny lights coming up at me from the ground. I grabbed the mitt from behind the captain's seat and put it on my right hand. Holding the support bar locked into the floor, I leaned out and grabbed the barrel, giving it a right turn. It was tighter than I thought it was going to be, but it came out. I brought the barrel back in and gave it to my crew chief, who exchanged it for a new barrel. Out, I went, once more, to put in the new barrel, but this one didn't want to go in as quickly. Now what?

I saw the captain urging me on to, "... hurry up, get it done. Those guys depend on us."

"No shit," I said to myself. I turned to my crew chief for help. He handed me the wrench we use when pulling maintenance.

"Give a tap on the tip, then try and turn it in," he said.

I did what he told me to do, and the barrel went in. I got back on my seat and radioed him to ask,

"What are all those lights coming up at us?"

Chili, my crew chief, looked blankly at me and said,

"Tracers! Keep shooting!"

I immediately went back to work. I didn't know what tracers looked like when they were coming up at you. I did see one or two go by on my left and my right. I also heard tink, tink, tink of rounds hitting the bottom of the ship. With both the 60s now working at max capacity and my 60 pumping out, I was amazed Charlie had time to stick his head up and shoot back. We supported ground troops hitting a village; that was our mission; it was over in half an hour. The ground commander gave us a thank you, and we were headed back to base. The pilot radioed,

"Nice work, men. Let's head home." The crew chief radioed the captain, "Good deal, sir."

Any involvement with Charlie was never very far from the camp, maybe 5 to 7 klicks. It only took us 5 to 10 minutes to get where we were needed. Sometimes a company of soldiers would need back-up while they were pinned down. We were often called to support med-evac ships picking up wounded men.

On one ferry mission, we were flying a prisoner down to Saigon for questioning. While idling on the PSP, two MP's (Military Police) walked up to the ship carrying a very small Vietnamese man dressed only in black silk pajama bottoms, no shirt, handcuffed behind his back. The MP's picked him up and threw the little guy onto the rugged aluminum deck of the ship, where he knocked his head loud enough for me to hear through my headset. It sounded like he cracked his head open. I reeled back and felt sorry for the guy. We didn't secure him with a seat belt or tie him down. We flew to

Saigon and turned him over to other MPs, then headed back to base. I thought, "Such inhumanity!"

Some days we kept busy, sun-up to sundown, and sometimes into the evening. On other days, with little to do, we searched for relief from the relentless Vietnam heat. As part of a gunship crew, you are never far from your ship. Relief, shade is often under the ship. You pray the siren would go off so you could do some flying, with or without combat. Charlie is an elusive little bastard. With so many long tunnels under the base, Charlie can duck back into them whenever he hears us coming. We don't always see him do it, so a flight becomes a sightseeing mission.

Our assignments had us waiting to be called into action. The ships were always prepped and ready to go. The guns were cleaned and prepped for loading at any time. There were 2500 rounds for the crew chief and 2500 rounds for me; almost 5000 rounds for the quad-60's. We didn't need anymore. The pods hanging under the quad-60's held nine rockets each, in a mix of HE (high explosive) and WP (white phosphorous). The radios were working well, something they didn't always do. When a mission is complete, you sit back and relax, wait and take a nap under the ship. Some guys dig into their c-rations looking for that Hershey's chocolate bar everybody loves. Then the siren goes off, and the opera begins again.

You drop what you're doing, no matter what. Grab your helmet, your flak jacket and jump into your seat; plug in your radio and check communications with your crew chief. By this time, the pilot and co-pilot have boarded with orders to where we are going. They are seated and have checked their radios with you. They fire up the ship, check the gages, wait for the blades to come up to speed, then lift off. The chief crew checks with the pilot, "Where to, this time, sir?"

"Seems the 5th (5th Mechanized Infantry) has got themselves in a jam trying to get Charlie out of a village. We've got to help them out. "Lock and load, check your guns. Watch for Charlie; he could be anywhere enroute."

It was late in the day, and the coming darkness was making it difficult to find targets. Flares were called in to be dropped by another by "Puff,"; a modified model C-47, fixed with mini-guns and flares. It was a very effective weapon. The G.I.'s called it, 'Puff the Magic Dragon,' and the men loved to see it do its thing, always a welcome sight.

We hovered at a safe altitude watching the armored units advance on the village. In time, a call came in from the commander of the 5th Mech to assist in the assault. We dove on a hut in the village after observing several men, in black pajamas, carrying AK-47s, enter. The co-pilot fired several rockets at the hut. The explosion made the roof rise in one piece while the walls folded inward, one by one.

"A house of cards," I said to myself.

We passed over the area witnessing several secondary explosions coming from inside the hut. The crew chief and I kept busy firing our 60's at running targets. APCs (Armored Personnel Carriers) from the 5th Mechanized Infantry, followed by an infantry unit, entered the village, capturing several VC and rounding up civilians. By all accounts, it was a successful mission. We headed back to base and made ready for another mission. All we needed was a little downtime to unwind from this one.

We flared into position and dropped into our revetment. Radios unplugged and helmets off, the -60s were down and ready for cleaning. I jumped off the ship and started inspecting for any bullet holes by way of Charlie. Sure enough, one passed by me and ended up in the transmission tunnel. We got lucky and didn't need any particular repair but a patch. I got lucky with my ammo can. It was under my left leg, under my seat, when I noticed a hole in the bottom of the ammo can. I showed my crew chief. He exclaimed,

"You are a lucky man, Bobby Boy. I don't know where that round landed, but we know it didn't hit you in the ass, which is where it should have ended up."

I stared at him, and the can and thanked God for that miss. We took a little time patching up the ship where it was needed, reloaded her, and got some rest. Talk among the aircrews was sometimes hilarious, sometimes scary as hell. Sitting in the EM club, over beers one sweltering afternoon, I heard one crew chief tell the story of how two black brothers had never been up in a helicopter before, and they wondered if they could get a ride. It seems they were thinking about becoming door gunners but needed to decide if they liked flying in a chopper with the door open. One of our best pilots got to take a ship up for the pleasure of the two men. He made the excuse he was taking the ship up as a check ride. With a crew chief and door gunner, the two, colored fellows jumped in and sat on the floor between the crew chief and the door gunner—neither of the brothers strapped in. The pilot lifted off, thinking his cargo was secure. Things don't generally slide out of a chopper unless the centrifugal force is missing, and it was missing on one of these poor guys. The story went on that the pilot was at 1000 ft when one of the men happened to slide out of the ship during a hard bank and fell into a rice paddy below. We laughed in doubt, saying that couldn't be true; it couldn't happen. Suspicion would have stayed with the story until that guy that fell out came by one afternoon to confirm the account. He survived with no serious injuries, but then he and his friend made the decision not to become door gunners. I believe they transferred into an Artillery unit.

Stories like that one didn't always end up in laughter. Many times, our ships, or those from other units, were used to interrogate VC prisoners. The practice was to take up two prisoners and ask one to talk. If he chose not to, he was thrown out of the helicopter. Seeing his buddy thrown from the ship, the other prisoner would become scared enough he would be very willing to answer any questions. It often worked. Personally, hating the enemy because he is the enemy does not preclude using some common decency. I didn't appreciate the practice of throwing someone off the ship any more than I did just throwing that little guy into the ship when he hit his head on the deck. But I found those sympathies don't go very far in a war zone. Most often, I would leave those kinds of incidences and go back to my hooch to get caught up on my letters and a little sleep.

CHAPTER 22

A Little Time Off

I had spare time one evening and decided to catch up on my writing. My first letter went to dad. I told of the mission and our success. I also told him of the man we lost and the one wounded. There was no holding back when I wrote to my father. I knew he understood how my days were, on and off the ship, especially the combat. My second letter went out to my big brother, Aaron, in Germany. He, too, got an earful of what was going on out here and what I was doing. His letters were always *'be careful: don't do anything stupid:'* those kinds of warnings. He knew I understood what he was saying, but he had to be the big brother and remind me, anyway.

Mom's letter was always longer than anyone else's, even my letters to Amanda. I always had to say something I could say to mom I wouldn't say to anyone else. Telling her of my life in Nam was a careful thing, delicate writing, different from my letters to dad or Art. But I felt free writing to mom. She could understand and accept anything I told her, and her best advice was said with love and caring, not a stern warning.

My letters to Amanda were filled with an eagerness to tell her how much I missed her. Of how I thought of her during the day and less of the dangers I faced in combat. I often drew sketches and pictures of houses we could build together when we got married. Yes, we discussed, quite heavily, a marriage. It wasn't going to be an expensive affair, but we wanted it to be memorable for everybody attending. She had it all planned out. It would be at the church in town. The reception would be at the Odd Fellows Hall so that we could save money. A family member belonged, so we saved some money there. All the guests would bring a dish, and the band was local. Amanda sent away to several honeymoon sites, near and away, that we might consider. I told her anything she planned would be alright with me. That always seemed to make right anything I might have said wrong.

After a couple of pages, I grabbed some sleep. The commotion in the hooch didn't wake me, only the siren from Charlie's mortar attack in the morning. It was 7:00 AM anyway, so I headed for the shower to start my day. Again, another cold shower.

"Somebody has got to fix that immersion heater," I told myself, heading back to the hooch.

Morning chow was welcome even though it was the usual serving of eggs, bacon, potatoes in one form or another. Hot Army coffee and a shovel full of SOS were a sure way to wake up. It was the SOS that got the morning going for you, filled with chipped beef, white sauce, and a desire to hit the head soon after.

As a crew member on a gunship, orders for extraneous duties were rare, but this one morning, my ship was down, and I had shit burning duty.

"Oh, the joy," I said to myself.

Now, shit-burning is not new science. Its been around for a while, many countries do it, and it's just as offensive elsewhere as it was in Nam. It only involves the removal of half a 55-gallon drum from under the asses of a lieutenant, and other officers, while they are seated in the outhouse. Believe me; their cheeks don't look any better than mine when they're sticking out the bottom of a "three-holer." But you drag the can aside, fill it with a mixture of aviation fuel and diesel, and lite it off. Then while it's burning, you stir the crap and the fuel to make sure it all burns completely.

Black smoke follows you no matter which way you turn. It gets into your uniform, your hair, even your mask if you have one, but it doesn't save you from the smell or the soot. By the time your duty is over, the shower is the first place you want to go. I was pleased not to get that duty very often. It was supposed to be rotational, but some men would be on duty as punishment.

Missions come and go every day, some hotter than others. Each mission would have you inspecting the ship afterward for bullet holes. I found one bullet hole that went through the transmission tunnel behind my seat. That same bullet just missed a hydraulic line, and that would have indeed brought the ship down into enemy territory.

On another mission, I examined the ammo can I placed under my seat, directly under my left thigh. For a second time, there was a hole in the bottom of the can where a round from an AK-47 came through the ship, entered the can, and disappeared. My crew chief and I searched for the spent round but couldn't find it. We were fortunate it didn't set off any of the other rounds in the can. I was lucky I didn't get hit in the leg.

Every mission held its kind of danger, whether just a ferry trip to Saigon with some men on vacation or full-blown combat against an enemy fighting in his backyard. Every time the ship lifted off the pad, and I sat fully exposed in the side door, all I wanted to see was the green and silver of the Vietnamese countryside. I could put aside the fifty-foot bomb craters leaving gaps in the carpet of green forest, but the mirror of the rice paddies in the morning sun could not be ignored. I was sure Vietnam was a beautiful country without a war going on.

CHAPTER 23

The Fate of the Brave

June 5, 1968, started the same as every day, hot. The humidity would creep up as the heat of the Asian sun filled the day. Typically, our morning mortaring by Charlie occurred at 0700. The rest of the day was spent keeping the ship ready for any alert. The crew was told to have our gear ready. '020', our ship, was on 'Stand By," waiting for that siren to go off at any time. I was a door gunner on Chili Rokes' ship this day. He and I had flown on several missions and had an excellent working rhythm going. By 1200 he was on the ship, making sure everything was ready. I asked him,

"Chili? Did you get any lunch?"

He yelled down from the engine deck, "Nah. I'll get something before the chow hall closes. I still have 15 minutes." He laughed. He was a good egg, easy to work with, suitable for a joke, and a fantastic crew chief. Chili knew his ship, upside down, backward, and forward.

He could fly a Huey if he had to move it around not too high off the ground, but he was not a certified pilot. He was a damn good crew chief, though, and I was proud to work with him.

The time spent working on the ship was worth it that afternoon. There were a few things, screws, torque tubes, control rods, that needed tweaking. The pilots liked their ships tight, with no sloppy linkage or leaking oil. Chili was always sure the ship was up to snuff; even the box of K-rations was full. We each had over 2500 rounds of 7.62, 3-in-1 ammunition. That means for every three rounds of ammo; there was a tracer. That made it easier for us to track a target. We also had a full, 24-count, 2.75 rocket load on each side of the ship, one pod on my side, one on Chili's side. The rockets were a mix of HE and WP, Proximity Rockets that exploded a predetermined height above the ground.

The ship also had an M-79 grenade launcher mounted on the nose. Like the hand-held M-79, this one was like a machine gun, pumping out grenades every second. It made a 'pumph-pumph-pumph,' sound as the rounds fired. We carried about 50 rounds, belt-fed, between Chili and me. They were fed between the pilot and the co-pilot, through to the nose to the gun out front. I heard some guys call it 'the Thumper.' It was guided by a remote targeting system, similar to how the quad-60s and the miniguns were aimed. Our Huey was a battleship in the air and ready. All we needed now was that siren to go off. Chili and I walked to the EM Club to cool down before any mission. NO beers, though. It was sodas only. We had to keep sharp. Any fuck-ups in the air could cost someone their life, and alcohol could easily cause any of us to make a fatal mistake.

It was late afternoon when the siren went off. Chili and I dropped our Cokes and headed for the ship. I passed the pilot, Chief Warrant Officer, W-3, Clay Johnson, along the way. That man, at the controls, was not afraid to fly the Huey like a sports car.

"Where are we going, sir?" I asked, on the run.

"The Mushroom." He said. He waved me on as if we were in a hurry.

I wasn't dogging it. I was in my seat, right behind him,

before he was. I looked over at Chili; we strapped in, connected our mics, and hung our -60's. Lt. Smitty Wayans, the pilot, pulled the ship up, out of the revetment, and Rokes and I locked and loaded our weapons as soon as we cleared the perimeter. Chili radioed the co-pilot,

"Where are we heading, Sir?"

"Upriver, about 10 klicks...a place called the Mushroom. It seems a couple of F-105's dropped a bomb or two, and only one exploded. They want us to detonate the other by firing on it. Sounds screwy to me, but we have to get to it before Charlie does."

The countryside of Viet Nam can be beautiful if you erase the bomb craters and the defoliated jungle from Agent Orange. The Saigon River meanders a long way, from the mountains in Cambodia to Saigon to the South China Sea, where the seacoast resort of Vong Tau is located. Vong Tau was the one place where VC and GI, alike, could enjoy the comforts of a seaside resort and forget about the fighting. I never got there, but I did get to fly the river once. Several missions back came to mind as we flew on.

It was a FireFly Mission, and the ship had a spotlight made of nine oversized high-intensity headlights, mounted on a frame that could tilt and swivel. The whole thing was bolted to the deck and pointed at any sampan or junk or barge on the river. They were not supposed to be out after dark. The Vietnamese people knew they had control of the river for fishing and other activities, but they were told not to use it at night. The Army found that Charlie was using the waterway to move weapons and VC to different fronts in the hope of coming up on our troops from behind.

Flying over the river, we would find a sampan headed south, possibly to Saigon, and we would fire upon it. Sometimes Charlie would fire back, sometimes not. But every mission resulted in an explosion on board the boat that would cause secondary explosions, telling us we made a good hit. The sampan was carrying weapons and munitions.

On other nighttime missions, we would be called to circle over an area where ground troops, embroiled in combat, needed light to find Charlie. We would kick flares out at one thousand feet, turning night into day for almost a minute. They would hang by their parachutes with a blinding white flare light, leaving the enemy exposed with his pants down, dead, or on the run.

But this mission was going to be different. We had to detonate a 500 lb. bomb from the air. That meant we had to shoot at it, which did not make a great deal of sense to me. From any safe distance above the bomb, even the shock wave would affect us in flight, and it would have to be a lucky shot in the first place to set it off. I hoped we were outside the blast radius.

We orbited at 800 ft when I last looked at the altimeter. The lead ship radioed he was going down to take a look. The pilot put the nose down and dove toward a hedge line. No one knew the exact location of the bomb because it was deep in the trees and elephant grass. He passed over at 100ft. and radioed back, immediately,

"Receiving fire, receiving fire." He pulled hard on the collective and climbed high to the right, taking hits all the way. Smitty kept our orbit at 800ft. and told me to pepper the area,

"Hard!" he ordered.

Firing over the rocket pod was a stretch on my part. I

got out as far as my monkey strap would go. Watching red and green tracers pass by me on the left and the right, I was hoping I wasn't in their way. With my last bullet expended, everything suddenly stopped and turned into a white void.

The following comes from the Duty Officer's Log, as reported by the pilot and witnesses on my ship...

"1810Hrs... Scramble LFT XT6032 contact Old Warrior 6, 230.10 or 69.85. DH2 LFT hit by unknown explosive. E-route 12th Evac, 1 WIA, 1855Hrs... Requested from ADAO if Old Warrior 6 will need replacement LFT. Cobras available. Old Warrior 6 says neg LFT needed 1945Hrs... EOD assessment of DH210, Gunship damaged, a large caliber rd, from outside source hit right rocket pod, exploding 1 rocket, Dislodging 2 rockets. Fragments cut Bungee Cord of M-60 and gun fell from A/C(aircraft) A/C received extensive skin damage. Rocket pod removed and will be destroyed."

My recollection continues.

I heard nothing, not a sound. I saw a white light, filled with confusion, lasting only a second or two. When it passed, I

knew something bad had happened, but I didn't know what. Then I looked down to check my legs. My left leg was still tucked under me, but my right, fully extended, as it was when I was firing, was not in good shape. I saw an open wound from my knee to the top of my boot. My leg was shattered. I shouted out one word,

"No! No!"

I turned to my left and caught my pilot eye to eye. Smitty simultaneously turned up the RPMs and headed back to base and the 12th Evacuation Hospital. I suddenly remembered my field training, "elevate the wound." I slipped off my seat and fell to the deck, placing my shattered leg on the edge of the seat. Blood was flying everywhere, getting in my eyes. I opened them to see Chili kneeling over me. He took off his monkey strap and wrapped it around my thigh as a tourniquet. I looked up into his face and told him, "Don't let me die, Rokes. Don't let me die." And I started praying harder than I have ever prayed before.

"Our Father, who art in heaven..."

Chili, with my blood splattering all over him, looked me in the face and said,

"You're not going to die, Bob. You're not going to die on me, not today!"

I reached up to touch the wound, trying to figure out how bad it was. The bones were splintered, shattered. The end, by my knee was sharp. I could feel flesh and muscle hanging off of it. Chili yelled at me,

"Don't touch it, Bob. We're getting you to the hospital as fast as we can. Don't worry; you're going to be alright."

I looked over my shoulder and could see the dash board gauges. The airspeed indicator was pegged past the red line. Looking back at Rokes, I felt the ship flair in preparation for landing. A team of doctors and nurses was waiting with a gurney. There was only one hold-up; the support rod between the roof and floor refused to unlock and release. It was held in by a slip and turn lock. While everyone fumbled to get it open, I just reached over and released it, as I had done a thousand times before. A male nurse grabbed me under the arms and placed me on the gurney and started to wheel me inside. A doctor looked at me; I looked at him and begged, "Don't take my leg, Doc. Please."

"Don't worry, son. I'm going to do all I can to save your leg."

I heard him tell a male nurse, "Stop that blood loss."

A black male nurse, the size of a linebacker, shoved his football-sized thumb into my groin to stop the bleeding. Just before passing out, I could feel something going back and forth across my leg. Darkness settled in.

I woke up in the middle of the afternoon the following day. I was in a ward of the 12th Evacuation Hospital on base. A pretty nurse was standing over me. She asked,

"How are we this morning?"

"What kind of question is that? Can't you see how I am? I'm lying here for a reason; don't you know that? Read my fuckin' chart!" I was not in the mood for a discussion on my well-being. I think I told her that in elevated tones.

She stuck a thermometer in my mouth, a blood pressure cuff on my arm, and a smile in my face. I knew how sincere two of those were, but I wasn't sure about the smile. She did her thing and scribbled on my chart. Then looked at me with a wider grin.

"The doctor will be with you soon. Sit tight."

I wanted to throw my bedpan at her, but I couldn't reach it. There were eight other men in the ward across from me, all with different injuries. One was out of bed pacing the floor, complaining about how he won't be able to play baseball with the Yankees. His arm was in a sling, and I thought of my legs. I raised my head to see how bad my right leg was. "Please, Lord, let my leg be okay, that the doctor didn't take it off." I could still feel it, so I wasn't worried. I slowly raised my head to see only one rise in the sheets where my two feet should be. Then I knew, and I wept, and wept, and wept. The ward went silent for a few moments until I heard one of the men across the way.

"Sure, you lost your leg, but you'll be walking again before long. I heard they can do some pretty neat things back in the world. Probably have you up and running in no time."

The soldier walking back and forth piped up loudly, "God, I hate this place. They can't even fix a simple wound so I can throw a baseball again. Fuck!" he exclaimed with a great deal of anger.

"You men can keep the noise down, if you don't mind," I heard the doctor say, walking in. He came to my bed and saw that I had been crying. "Does it hurt right now, son?"

"Did you have to take it off, doc? I asked you not to take it off, Doc," I pleaded.

"I had no choice, son. Your knee was gone, and the rest of your leg, you wouldn't be able to use it. It had to go. I'm sorry," he added, motioning for a nurse. I memorized his name tag, "Guyer."

"Give him something to help him sleep. I'll be back later today. Don't worry, son. We're going to take good care of you."

My eyes were closed as he left, and the nurse made sure they would be for a while. A couple of hours later the doctor was standing at my bedside again. I looked at him once and turned my head with a tear rolling down my cheek.

"I need to look at the wound, son. I'll be as gentle as I can." he unraveled the bandage and tossed the bloody one away, asking the nurse for a new one. He washed debris from the wound and told the nurse to arrange to get me on the next ride to Japan.

"Is that a bigger hospital, Doc?"

"Yes. Bigger and better. They'll be able to do more for you. Make sure he stays in bed, keep him quiet, not sedated. I'll see you again soon. Rest easy."

I had one visitor from the 25th, Ronnie. He told me about the condition of the ship. I wanted to know how much damage it had sustained in the explosion. I didn't know why, it didn't matter anymore. I still felt connected to her, just morbid curiosity, I guess.

"Hi, Ron," we shook hands like old friends, but the odd thing was he was new to the company, and I hardly knew him. I was surprised that anyone came to see me.

"Hey, Bob, how are you feeling?" There was a lot of sincerity in his voice, a comfort to know someone cared about what happened to me.

"What does the ship look like, Ronnie?"

"Oh, shit. It's all fucked up. The blades need replacing; we can't patch them. Do you know you lost your - 60?"

"What do you mean I lost my -60? It wasn't on the ship?"

"Nope. Top saw your bungee was cut. He thinks it went out the door when you got hit. Charlie's got it now."

"Fuck! I didn't know I dropped it."

"I found your helmet, though. The friction knob is missing, and you can't see out your face mask. It was completely speckled. I don't know why your face isn't marked up with shrapnel."

"No shit!" I exclaimed.

"Oh, yeah, and your monkey strap? It was cut in four places, behind you."

The Lieutenant and the C.O. can't figure out how that happened; four cuts behind you? That three-inch bundle of wires in the roof above your head was completely cut through.

"The ship is a mess, but don't worry about it. We'll fix it; 020 will fly again."

I told Ron what I saw in the explosion. He thought it was weird. I agreed. He spent about an hour with me and said,

"I have your name and address. I'm gonna look you up when I get home. That's a promise."

With that, we shook hands, and he left. The nurse brought In a dinner tray with fried chicken, biscuit with mashed potatoes, and gravy. They tasted good, too. It didn't take long for me to drift off again. Darkness came before supper, and a new patient was placed next to me. The first thing that opened my eyes was the smell. I knew what gangrene smelled like, but this was mixed with something rotten. I had the nurse lift the head of my bed so I could talk to the man. He had to be horribly wounded to smell so bad.

I thought my eyes were playing games with me, because I recognized the man. It was Al Robbins, the guy I talked with on the bus, more than a year ago. His eyes closed, I thought he might be asleep, so I just let him be. Then, I heard him speak, softly, barely audible.

"Hey, white boy!" he said.

"Al!" I exclaimed. "You remembered me?"

Of course, I do. How does anyone forget a guy whose ass got whipped so many times playing chess? How are you doing, Bob?"

I paused, looking at him and the shape he was in. Then I looked at myself and said, "Oh, no big thing, Al. Just a scratch." I couldn't give him a comparison. I thought that would be cruel.

"What happened, Al? Where the hell have you been?" He called for a nurse and asked for a cigarette. The nurse told him he shouldn't be smoking with the shape he was in.

"Aw, come on. I don't need that shit-talk. Who knows how many more I'm gonna get. "

One of the men across the ward gave her a Pall Mall. I was surprised it happened to be the complaining Jersey boy that wasn't going to play baseball anymore. I looked at him, he smiled with some kind of apology. The nurse brought the cigarette to Al and stood by his bed while he smoked. He took one long drag and blew out a blue-white cloud.

"When I hit country, they had me working in the motor pool. I got sick of pulling wrenches, you know. I told my sergeant I was an APC driver and wanted a transfer to the CAV. The Old Man brought me the papers; the next thing I know, I'm in the 11th CAV, on top my APC, and sitting on a headstone. They needed me."

He called for another drag. The nurse obliged then sat to listen to more of Al's story.

"Sittin' on a headstone," I said. "I heard that before."

"Yeah," he said. "Aren't we all just sittin on a

headstone somewhere out there?" he pointed with his stumpy hand. "It's all the same shit, man. In the bush, a chopper, a tank; it's all the same shit. We're all sittin' on a headstone."

"So, what happened to you?" I asked.

"We were chasing Charlie and had him boxed in, not far from the Mountain. We followed him into a vill. I was going over a bridge when the fuckin' thing let go, and my ride got stuck. We couldn't move, and Charlie had us dead to rights. He's peppering my ride all to hell. Me and the gunner decided to di-di-mow. We couldn't wait for anybody. He bought it jumping off the top. I followed up to get my ass out when I spotted an RPG came in at us. It came through the side and blew me out, up through the hatch. A corpsman found me in this shit-filled stream."

The nurse gave Al the last drag of his cigarette. He twisted and writhed a bit. "Need a little morphine, Al?"

"Yeah," he said, grimacing in pain, "I need something. You got any weed?" We all laughed.

The doctor came in and ordered a drip for Al. He heard Al ask for the weed. "I'm sorry, son, but if the hospital had any marijuana, everyone here would be fighting over it." He checked the wound on, what should have been Al's right arm. It was missing at the elbow; one eye remained, but it was barely usable. His left hand was heavily bandaged from several bullet wounds. The doctor asked the nurse to help turn Al over to check the shrapnel wounds he suffered in his back. All I could see was raw meat, no holes from shrapnel. The doctor placed a clean absorbent pad under Al and gently placed him back down on his back. He looked at Al and told him,

"I'll address those back wounds as soon as I can, soldier. Tell the nurse if you need any pain meds; just let us know."

Al responded, "Thanks, Doc."

The nurse looked at Al with a sad face. It was the first time she didn't have a smile. Al said to her,

"Don't worry, sweetheart. The doc will have me fixed up soon enough. Right now, I could use another cigarette."

I couldn't understand how Al survived such trauma and wounding. His attitude and posture on it all were the finest example of positivity I had ever come across. The shot didn't take long to put Al to sleep. He went out before his cigarette.

Two nurses went to work cleaning Al's gangrenous wounds. The smell of those wounds was horrible, but Al wouldn't stand a chance in hell of making it home without surgery. Their severity would surely bring on a poison that would kill him. There was no comparison between Al's wounds and the other soldiers in the ward, not even mine. The doctors and nurses considered Al alive but not for much longer. When he was awake, Al and I made the most of the time we could together, just talking.

One nurse stayed at Al's bedside through the supper hour and past curfew. I dropped off and awoke the following morning to the same nurse sitting by Al's bed.

C H A P T E R 2 4

The Medicine of Healing

"How's he doing?" I whispered.

"He hasn't stirred all night. The doctor should be in shortly."

My nurse came in to check my drips and popped a thermometer in my mouth. When she pulled it out and read 104 she scrambled a team to come in and pack me with ice. They noticed my right arm was bent over my head kinking the line of the I.V. That movement had cut the supply of fluids I needed, the fluids I had lost in the wounding and the surgery. Four nurses rushed in with ice pack for every warm spot on my body. I had an ice pack under each arm two in my groin, two behind my neck and a fresh ivy in my arm.

One nurse looked at me and told me, "Don't do that again."

The doctor ran in and told me to keep my arms down so they can replace the fluids I lost. I answered,

"Ok."

The rest of the day passed quietly. I watched the nurses take Al into the operating room. He didn't return while I was still there. It was almost supper time when two male nurses handed me my chart, telling me,

127

"Don't lose these." They took me out of bed placed me in a wheelchair and rolled me out to a waiting C-130 transport. I was gone and in the air before I knew where I was going. Strapped into the wheelchair and the chair fastened to the floor of the plane I felt every bump and air current the plane hit. The best I knew, I was 'getting out of Dodge' and Viet Nam. There was no time to say goodbye to Al.

The flight wasn't a long one. I had a nurse watching my temperature and blood pressure all the way. She gave me juice to drink before we touched down in Japan. With no window seat, I didn't know what Japan looked like before we landed. It was late evening, and I didn't get any better view after they dropped the ramp. A couple of nurses ran out from the hospital, grabbed my wheelchair, and ran me into the operating room. There was no time for explanations, questions or answers.

The following day, when I woke up in my bed the doctor kept me away from other patients because my wound was still open. He didn't want to risk infection setting in. A male nurse came in to ask the ever popular, "How are we this morning?"

I looked up at him and answered, "I don't know about you, but I feel like shit. What did you guys do to me?"

"You started running a fever on the flight over, so they ran you up here to the operating room to make sure everything was alright."

"Is it?" I asked.

"Let's say we want to avoid any further complications. The operation was to make sure you didn't have an infection, but they also wanted to find out what was causing your temperature to spike."

"Did it have anything to do with that bent arm thing that backed up all my fluids? They packed me in ice from the crotch to my armpits to bring down my temperature."

"No, I don't think so. But whatever, you'll get a light breakfast to see if you keep it down. After that, we'll see how things go with your temp and blood pressure. Does your leg hurt at all?"

"Yeah, it's starting to ache and itch, too," I told him.

"That all from the surgery. I'll be in later to clean that wound. Breakfast will be right in."

"Hey, can you find out how Al Robbins made out? He was at the 12th Evac., right next to me. Black fella, with the CAV. He got pretty messed up." I had to know about Al, whether or not he made it."

"Al Robbins? Alright. I'll check. I know somebody at the 12th. I'll give him a call this afternoon."

"Hey, thanks a lot." I hoped I would have an answer soon. The actions of the doctors and the nurses attending Al weren't too positive. It appeared to me all they wanted to do was relieve his pain.

One of the personnel from the kitchen brought out a small bowl of oatmeal, I think; two pieces of toast, no butter, and half a cup of coffee, room temperature. I ate because I was hungry, but it didn't stay with me long. Just as the male nurse came in to check on my progress, I found the bedpan and loaded it with my oatmeal. The nurse quickly ran to my side to offer his version of comfort.

What can anyone do? What kind of comfort is synonymous with vomiting? He took the bedpan before I finished with it. He didn't get very far. I was amazed at how much I had in me. The bedpan was full, and the nurse was turning yellow. He passed the bedpan to a female nurse assisting him.

"Would you empty this, please?"

"Sure," she said.

"Her stomach is stronger than yours'" I told him.

"This morning it is. How do you feel now?"

"Hungry."

He laughed. "More will come later. The meds from surgery can play with your stomach and appetite. I think you'll be okay for lunch. I'll come back and check later. Sit tight; I'm going to change your dressing."

He then went off and gathered what he needed to flush my wound. When he returned, he unwrapped the bandage around my stump. It would be the first time I would see what the doctor in Viet Nam did to my leg. As the nurse peeled back the final piece of gauze bandage, I could feel the air conditioning in the room. My stump felt the coolness rushing over the open wound. It was a large incision, from the end of my stump, up to the inside of my leg, stopping a few inches from my balls.

So, that's what he did. I'm glad he didn't go any farther up."

"Looks like he didn't have to. This is a good-looking wound, nice and clean, no ragged edges."

He turned around to his rolling table and grabbed a bottle of hydrogen peroxide and a couple of long swabs, the ones on a stick. He warned me, "This might sting a bit. If you feel dizzy, lie back."

I remained sitting up and watched him slowly pour the peroxide on my open wound. I didn't feel anything until he started rubbing the swabs across the open muscle, and then, I could feel the swab, but lightly.

"Wow," I told him. "That's the inside of my leg, huh?"

"Yes, the doctor did a good job. He saved quite a bit of your leg, considering what I read of the initial report. You're a lucky guy, Mister."

"Yeah. I'm a lucky guy," then I lay down in my bed and

started to cry. I had nothing to say to him. I could only think, I had lost my leg. Now, what am I going to do?

"It's a shock, I know. I've seen it from a lot of guys—some with injuries worse than yours', some not as bad. But you're going home. You're going to learn to walk again, and you'll be able to make a life for yourself. Uncle Sam will help you. It may take a little while, but you'll make it."

I could feel the empathy, the sincerity, but right then, right there, it all sounded like bullshit. It was my leg, my life, that got fucked up, and I was the one that had to fight my way back.

The nurse finished cleaning the wound and asked if I wanted anything to help me sleep.

"Yeah. It's starting to ache."

"I'll get you something."

He was back in fifteen minutes. I was fighting the pain, waiting for that shot. I asked, "Were you able to find out anything about my buddy, Al Robbins?"

Yeah, I just got the call. That's why it took me so long to get back to you." He lowered his head and told me, "He didn't make it."

Now I could feel a pain in my chest with Al's death. I started to tear up when the nurse offered an 'I'm sorry.' He then gave me the shot and the pain disappeared and I filled my head with dreams of Al and I laying chess on the train.

CHAPTER 25

Al's Mark

I woke around lunchtime and got into my wheelchair, feeling I had to find a way to deal with Al's death. I didn't know Al, really. We hadn't seen one another for more than a year. Oddly enough, he was with the 5th Mech, assigned to the 25th. He was living on the Base. Somehow, we lost track of one another and never realized we were living in the same neighborhood.

We could have been good friends if only we had thought of searching each other out. That we had forgotten, we were both stationed on the same base, with the same Division.

I had not met another black soldier like Al while in the Division, not at the 725th Maintenance or the 25th Aviation, my gunship company. He struck me as someone I could trust, depend on, had my back. I got all that from playing chess on a bus ride, losing every match. He had a great smile, a positive attitude, and a polite manner. He always let me go first when playing chess, and he did it with grace, a gentlemanly kind of grace.

God bless you, Al. I'm going to miss a good friend.

CHAPTER 26

A Long Way Home

I decided to tour the hallways and see just how big this hospital was. It was more than a MASH unit. The branches of the wards went out everywhere. Rolling down one hallway, I peeked into one ward. I was struck funny by what I saw. The ward was large; I guess it held 30 or 40 beds, 20 on each side. The funny part was that every man and woman had one leg up in traction, all in the same pose, almost as if they were saluting the flag or someone. The ward was quiet, so I didn't go in. I backed away from the door and went rolling in another direction. I didn't stray too far from my ward, no matter where I went; it was all the same. I rolled back to mine and got back in bed. Lunch was coming anyway.

Those were my days in the hospital in Japan. Not exciting, the same wrap and wrap, and flushing of my wound. I did wake up one day, and two nurses came in to wheel me out of my ward and into the OR.

"What's going on? What are you going to do to me today?" I asked with a bit of anticipation.

"The doctor wants a closer examination. He may even close the wound today and get you ready to go home."

My male nurse hadn't said anything to me about going home. After three weeks as a guest in Japan, I wanted to go home. As it happened, I wasn't watching the clock or the calendar in Nam when I got hit. I wasn't watching here either in Japan. Time was irrelevant to me; day, night, breakfast, lunch, or dinner, they passed every day, and so did I. It was just a matter of how many magazines I could read or how much Armed Forces Television I could stand to watch. I was always back in my room by supper, every night, after roaming the halls.

My nurse came in to tell me the doctor would be in to see me after dinner. He stood there with a grin on his face then said, "You're leaving us."

"When? Am I going home? I don't know if I'm ready for home yet; not like this."

"I don't know where you're going, but you are leaving this evening to a stateside hospital, another Army base."

No sooner had he told me when the doctor walked in.

"Mr. Lemon?" he asked. They never used my rank to address me. I wondered why. He began telling me my wound was in good shape. He closed it this afternoon so that I could make the trip this evening. Ft. Bragg Army Hospital was my next stop, and that I could expect more surgery when I got there.

"Okay. When do I leave?" I asked.

"In about ten minutes." He told the nurse to get me ready and promptly left.

"He didn't say goodbye?" I asked.

"They never do. Good luck, Bob," were his last words to me. I was placed on a gurney, and a nurse on the flight came in and rolled me up into the C-141 Starlifter. Three attendants on the plane lifted me high into the last bunk at the highest place in the tail of the plane. I could look down and see the loading ramp. There was a tiny glass portal, a 6 X 8 oval, that I could see the night sky. This plane was a lot different than the one I rode in getting to Nam. There were no padded seats for anyone except the crew, I supposed. The takeoff was short and very loud. There was no report from the pilot about our altitude or cruising speed, no seat belt or no smoking signs. It was just a modern-day Mayflower, filled with patients, on a return trip home. Nurses and crew came around with a brown-bag lunch and a can of Coke for everyone. I can't remember what kind of sandwich I had, but I do remember one patient saying,

"As far as taste is concerned, this stuff is designed more to keep our bowels moving rather than fill our stomachs."

He may have been right. The Coke wasn't cold, the sandwich was dry, and the cookie was wrapped in cellophane. I fell asleep after my meal and awoke to the tires screaming as they hit the tarmac of Pope Field, outside Ft. Bragg. Nurses and orderlies came out to greet us and take us directly into the hospital. I heard one nurse say,

"This one is spiking a fever. Get him to O.R., right away."

So, off I went to surgery again. A minor thing, I found. I had gone too long between wound cleanings. But the doctor did say he was scheduling me for major surgery to redress the end of my stump. I guessed they didn't like the way it looked on my X-Rays.

When I awoke from surgery, I found my mother and father standing at the foot of my bed. I could have gone into shock, "Mom, Dad, what are you doing here?" Then I saw my aunt and uncle had also come with them.

"Wow, what a surprise." Then I saw dad walk away. Mom made the excuse he went out for a cigarette, but I saw him wiping his eyes as he turned. I knew he was upset at seeing his son with only one leg. That was in August of '68. Mom told me, Lorraine was getting married in September. She asked if I might be able to get home for that. I told her I would ask the doctor. I was still in the Army, so it would have to be chalked up to leave time. I said I would try.

Our conversation was light, and most of it revolved around home and my brothers and sisters. When it came time to leave dad, and my uncle came back in. Dad hugged me with a tear in his eye. I told him, "It's okay, dad. I'll be okay. They're going to teach me to walk again, wait and see."

His answer was, "I know, son. I know. I'll see you when you get home." With that, he left mom to make the goodbyes. She told me they were staying at a motel nearby and would return in a day or two. Dad didn't want to come back to see me, and I understood. He taught me that while I was growing up. He didn't know how much he prepared me for war or the eventuality of suffering as a result. Somehow, I knew something was going to happen. I just didn't bargain on anything as big as losing a leg. I guess no soldier does.

Writing to Amanda took a back seat for a while. I didn't know how to tell her I was wounded or had suffered the loss of a leg. I had to tell her it was in action but didn't want to say how bad. Mentioning Japan then Ft. Bragg, she wasn't sure where I was or would be next. I wrote to her when I got home, even called her, just to hear her voice. Her letters were a heartbreak to me, her emotions bleeding like wet ink on paper. I cried to read them. Everything we talked about was now put on hold, the engagement, the wedding, the honeymoon. It all seemed so far away now. But she wrote like she was willing to wait, so I accepted that. It felt like my doubts were gone. Suddenly there was a new purpose in learning to walk again and as quickly as possible. But I had to wait for the Army to let me go and become a civilian again so I could wipe away any time schedules the government might decide to put on me.

I approached my doctor and explained my desire to get home for my sister's September wedding. Once he looked over my chart and made sure my healing progress met his standards, he consented. I told my mom and dad. They said they would arrange to pick me up from wherever I arrived. I made my plans right away. The Hospital helped secure a ride for me. I caught a hop aboard a DC-3 to the subbase in Groton.

Carrying no more than a weekender bag on crutches, I was able to board the plane and enjoy the ride to Groton. The crew of the DC-3 gave me a hand getting on and off the plane. The cab driver helped me into his cab and took me to the train station. I caught him peeking back at me during the ride. He commented,

"I feel for you, son; wounded and all. But I got to tell you," He shook his head emphatically.

"I do not agree with this war, no sir, not one bit." He didn't say any more; he just kept looking back at me. Our eyes met for one moment, and I told him,

"Everybody's got opinions about the war; some approve, some don't, but I joined the Army. I wasn't drafted, and that means I take orders, even orders to go to war. But honestly, I don't agree with this war, either."

The rest of the ride to the train station was quiet. The driver helped me out of the cab and led me to a bench near the ticket window. I held up his fare; he wouldn't take it. He told me,

"I wish you luck, son. I hope you get to make something of your life and don't get stuck living off an Army pension. You keep the fare. I've got a feeling you're going to need it more than me."

I said, "Thank you. Have a good day."

The cabby walked two steps, turned, and offered a salute. I saluted back, then watched the cab drive away. I had to wipe my eyes before I went to the counter to buy my train ticket to Providence. I've always been the patriotic kind of guy. That cabby hit me in the right place. I wondered how many other folks would act as he did.

With ticket in hand, I made my way to the boarding platform. It was an uncomfortable feeling, sitting there. People would notice the uniform first, then the crutches, then the reason for the crutches. I couldn't believe how far they would walk to find a bench before boarding the train.

Passengers would walk away from this man in uniform. I think, wounded or not, they saw a soldier who probably served in Viet Nam and killed all those women and children. I felt like an outcast and could only blame the news about Mi Lai and Lt. Calley.

"How dare they equate all of us serving in Viet Nam were like that? Why blame me personally?" I thought. I was ready to throw my crutches at them, but I held back and turned my back on them.

"What did they know about the cost of freedom? About how many men were dying every day? How much blood was shed for them?" I was seething inside and felt this trip was going to be a long one.

The conductor was the only person to help me down on and off the train. It was only an hour ride but an uncomfortable one. Two seats in front of me, a mother got up and moved, taking her young son up five more seats and to the other side of the aisle.

"No patriotism in your heart, aye, lady," I said to myself. She didn't hear me, and just as well. I was in the mood to let someone have it, but I wasn't willing to let a woman with her child feel the brunt of my anger.

Getting off the train wasn't any easier than getting on.

The porter on the platform was there to lend me a hand. I spotted my father and uncle waving, waiting for me. Dad came up to me and fathered a manly hug, as did my uncle, both of them, drunk as a skunk, neither of them fit to drive. But since my uncle was aiding dad, my uncle got behind the wheel and drove the 25 miles to my sisters' wedding reception. What a ride. I was more afraid in the back seat of my uncle's Dodge than sittin' on that headstone in the Huey. In both cases, I prayed to God, we made it through to the end of the ride. That was my way of knowing life would begin again. We made it to the reception, where my brother Arthur greeted me. He came up and eagerly offered a big hug and assistance into St. John's Hall.

"Brother,' He said. "Let me give you a hand, maybe a leg, up these steps." That was Arthur, always a good word on the funny side.

"Any help from you, Art, is a pleasure, indeed. Thanks."

We made it into the hall, where family and friends immediately mobbed me. There were hugs, kisses, tears, all the emotion a guy could ever want. My mother was first with her tears, followed by my brother with a rolling chair. Then came my grandmothers, tears flowing. My grandfather came up with a handshake and a hearty pat on the back. Arthur pushed my chair to a table with the biggest piece of wedding cake and a cup of coffee. There were relatives at the wedding I hadn't seen in years; others I had never met. They all knew I was going to be there. Now they were seeing a wounded soldier.

"Oh, the poor boy," some said.

"Is there anything I can do for you?" others asked.

My younger brothers and sisters weren't sure what to make of their older brother, this man in uniform with one leg. It went on until my sister introduced me to her husband, "Bob, this is Ned. Ned, my brother Bob."

We did the 'hello's, how are you, you're going to treat my sister well, or I'm going to kill you,' sort of thing. I had a drink and a piece of wedding cake. The attention was overwhelming until my big brother came by with his sense of composure and asked,

"Are you tired, little brother?" He always seemed to own the feeling of calm and composition, not guru-like, but he could play one in Hollywood. That was one of the things I loved about my brother, Aaron. He always drew me to want to be around him. We sat and talked of minor things for a little while until fatigue started to take over. The real work of getting on and off the plane, the train, and the length of the trip; was arduous. Perhaps I left the hospital too soon, or maybe I needed another drink and another piece of wedding cake. Either way, I was running out of steam having a hard time dealing with the crowd. I asked him to drive me home.

"Where? South Carolina?" he asked, jokingly. That was his sense of humor.

"No, fool. Ma's house." I retorted.

"I know," he answered, "Come on, I'll help you up." I loved his empathy. I could feel how much he cared.

The house was just down the hill, where we grew up, walked to and from first grade, and all our classes together. Why do memories make tears? Why can't they stay back there, in that hollow designed for them, in your brain, and let the future go on? Our service times brought us close. Perhaps this incident would bring us closer, for a little while, anyway. Arthur helped me up the three granite steps into the house and onto the sofa.

"Here you go, brother. Comfortable?"

"Yeah, this is good for now. Thanks, Art."

"Do you want anything, a drink of water, a cigarette, a kick in the ass?" He was referring to my wounding and the insane decision

I made getting there. We had discussed it earlier, and the decision remained mine to the end.

"You can save the kick in the ass until I'm walking again, thanks. Nothing else; I'll lie here till the others get back. Thanks. You go back, enjoy the crowd. Have another drink with our new brother-in-law and watch your pockets."

"OOH! Good one," Art exclaimed. He knew what I meant. Lory had married into a different culture, and it would take a little time for any of us to get used to him. Ned came from a fishing village on the coast, south of Boston, New Bedford; nice place, lots of fishermen. They talked funny, ate, and lived differently, kind of "cliquey." I wondered if it was because he was a lawyer. Some of us thought suspiciously of him, a lawyer from a fishing village. Lory said he was quite a catch. I wasn't sure I should laugh at that one, but I tried.

Mom was home in about an hour. I asked her to give me a hand changing the bandage the doctor had last put on my wound. I was growing concerned about it. Not because it had been on longer than I anticipated, but that it was starting to smell. I removed the old bandage and saw the color was good. The wound itself was a small opening at the end of my stump. The doctor said it was to close from the inside out and that it was still draining. That was why I still had a bandage, but he didn't say anything about an odor. I told mom, "That's not a good smell, ma."

"Yes, it does smell bad. What do you want me to do?" she asked.

"I think I should go to the VA in Providence. This is infected from something and needs to be taken care of right away."

She helped me bandage the wound for traveling, and we made our way to the hospital. Providence was only 40 minutes from the Village, and the road was a major thorough fair. Mom pulled up in front of the hospital. As I hobbled my way in on crutches, I no sooner had gotten through the door when the chief Surgeon, just getting off the elevator, told the nurse at the desk, "Get this man up to OR. Now."

He looked at my mother and told her,

"Your son has a major infection, mam. I could smell it as soon as I got off the elevator. I'm going to find out what and where it is, and I'm going to take care of it. Don't worry. I'll take good care of him. Have a seat in the waiting room. I'll be keeping in touch as I progress through the operation." With that, he was off to the OR.

Mom was led to the waiting room and offered, "Can I get you anything, Mrs. Lemon?"

Mom answered, "Can I get a cup of coffee, black, please?"

"Of course. I'll be right back."

An aide was back in 5 minutes. "Here you are, mam. Is it all right?"

"Yes. Thank you." Mom was always welcome to a good cup of black coffee.

It's funny how you never welcome the feel of a gurney. They're the same no matter which operating room you visit. The prep room is always cold. Outside it was early September. In the O.R., it was the middle of January.

X-rays showed me what was causing the infection. Two large pieces of shrapnel were lodged themselves high in my groin area and had escaped the eyes of the Army surgeons. I must have had five or six visits with them, and no one could find it. I recognized those two pieces as coming from the rocket that exploded in front of me on June 5.

The doctor came in just as I was about to drop off, and I think he said, don't w-o-r-r-y, s—o—n..."

The operation lasted over an hour. When the doctor finished, he spoke with my mother. She was still holding her coffee and saying a Rosary.

"Mrs. Lemon? Your son is going to be alright. We found out what was wrong. He had two pieces of shrapnel still in his leg. The Army missed them because they couldn't see them. I took them out and cleaned up the wound. It's closed, partially, and will have to close completely from the inside out. He will have an irrigation hole that will keep the wound draining to stem off any further infection. I think he'll be able to go home in a couple of days. We are going to notify the Army and let them know he's here and what has happened. From there, it's up to them. I suspect your son will be transferred to another Army hospital. You can go up to see him in about 30 minutes. An aide will come down to help you."

"Thank you, doctor, thank you very much."

Mom was sitting at my bedside with her Rosary when I opened my eyes. The grogginess was gone, and my eyes focused on my beautiful mother. "Hi, Mom."

She was ready with a kiss before I opened my mouth. "How are you feeling, son?"

"I think I'm doing alright, now. That little bit of discomfort I had is gone. I guess you saw the doctor."

"Yes. The doctor came down to see me and told me what was causing the infection. You still had two big pieces of metal in you. The other doctors couldn't see them. But they're gone now. The doctor says you're going to be okay."

"When I was in the Operating Room, I saw the X-Ray they took. It showed two pieces of the rocket that exploded when I got hit. I recognized them right away."

Mom looked a bit upset as I was explaining what I saw. I knew mom was a champ. She could take a lot, especially after having nine kids. You need to come out strong. I guess that's why I found it so easy to talk to her; dad wasn't so easy. His military approach got hard, sometimes. It was challenging making him understand. He was a matter-of-fact person, no beating around the bush, get to it, and no bull shit. That was how dad handled everything. Mom never let herself get that way. Her soft side was a welcome retreat from dad's demeanor. But I loved them both. How could I not?

The doctor came in and told me all the things he did, how he made this change, and fixed that part. I didn't have to understand him. I only had to thank him. He told me the VA notified the Army I was in the hospital and for what reason. Then dropped the hammer to say I would be leaving as soon as I was able. I could go home for a while, but orders were coming down for me to either go back to Bragg or to another Army hospital in the area. Given a choice, an

Army hospital in Massachusetts was only an hour away. In less than a month, I was told to report to Ft. Devens Army Hospital.

I had to stay 'in the Army' while I recuperated, and the Army brass had to decide what to do with me, 'officially;' It took them four months to decide I was to go back to the VA in Providence to learn to walk again. I went to a brace shop outside of Boston to see a man who would make a new leg for me. The excitement raced through me. "This is going to be great," I thought.

And all this time; the trip from Nam to Bragg; subsequent operation after operation; dealing with the infection. I was still writing to Amanda to keep her updated and let her know I hadn't forgotten about her. She said that plans for a wedding were moving forward and that she couldn't wait to see me again. I thought, for sure, she was going to tell me to hit the road after losing my leg. I had to call her from the hospital to tell her I was happy to hear her voice and not stop writing.

CHAPTER 27

A New Life Beginning

Our wedding coming up was the impetus for me to walk out of Providence, VA, in May of '69. My strength and determination to walk again made taking the pain of learning to use my new leg easier to bear. It was complex learning to step and manipulate a cane and the new leg together. The assistance I received from the VA and the people that made the prosthesis was top-notch. The man who made my new leg wore one himself, which positively contributed to my motivation. My stability and confidence would grow in time, and the wedding was coming up in July.

My mother and father, several aunts and uncles, and brothers and sisters flew down to West Virginia for the weekend affair. It was a grand time, and everyone truly enjoyed themselves. Amanda's parents got along very well with my parents. I think my father and Amanda's father exchanged more drinks and salutations than there were bottles on the bar. My mother danced with me and told me she was very happy for us, and she felt I had made a good choice. My dad loved Amanda right away and was waiting to take her into the family in Rhode Island like a daughter. Dad felt sorry for Amanda's folks and her brothers and sisters because I was taking her away from them. He wanted our Rhode Island family to grow, but dad, and Amanda's family, understood the promise that we would gladly visit from time to time. Rhode Island was going to be our home, and Amanda was more than willing to leave the coal mines of West Virginia for the quaintness of a Rhode Island town.

We had a brief, sweet honeymoon in the Blue Ridge Mountains before settling into an apartment north of Providence. My G.I. Bill helped me attend a school in design and architecture while Amanda searched for work. She was able to find employment in an upscale furniture and appliance showroom.

It didn't take long before the Langdon proclivity for growing families began to occur. Within nine months of our vows, Amanda was pregnant. I was as happy as an expectant father could be, but Amanda was feeling something different. She said she wasn't ready to start raising a family. My heart reeled as it did when Joan left me. We had made a home in No. Providence, preparing to start a family, and now this. We both took our Catholic upbringing seriously, so there was no alternative to keeping the baby and following through with the pregnancy. Amanda's concern was her appearance through it all; looking 'weird,' not 'right' with everybody; feeling temperamental and argumentative. My argument to her was that she would look beautiful. A lot I knew. Not all women want to look fat and bulbous through a nine-month progressive calendar.

We eventually survived the expansion and contraction of Amanda's abdomen, and our first child, a girl, and Kylie was born. She was a cranky baby. We didn't know if it was the formula or colic; maybe it was Amanda or me she didn't like. We didn't know what to do on all those crying nights. One of us had to stay up with her until she fell asleep. Amanda figured that if she worked all day and I didn't, I was supposed to stay up with her all night; I did.

It took a couple of months before we were indeed able to enjoy having Kylie around. There were nights when we both wanted to close the door and let her cry herself to sleep, but I couldn't do that for very long. Getting up, I often fell asleep with her in my arms, in the rocking chair my parents gave us. What a godsend that was. I used it often with Kylie and alone. Time to adjust to the surroundings was what Kylie needed. In time we all fell into a place of harmony and began enjoying each other, the apartment, and the neighborhood.

I began feeling a change was needed on my road to some career path. I wanted to go to school to learn to fly and get into the aviation industry. I talked to the VA about my disability benefits, and they told me schooling was one benefit I should take advantage of. The school I had in mind was in New Hampshire; it wasn't a big school, but it offered all the curriculum I needed to set me in the right direction. It also had a small airfield with several small Piper and Cessna aircraft. I impatiently waited for the paperwork between the VA and the school to be completed.

I was reading positive signs in my dreams. Flying all over the place, and New Hampshire looked like it would be the place to make all those dreams come true. My last attempt at schooling, in Providence, for Architectural Engineering kept getting snagged in government paperwork. My attempts to use my G.I. Bill were not very successful. I told Uncle Sam no more and dropped out of school. I was doing very well with my studies but not very well with the government. I dropped out of my architectural classes and went back into the work-a-day world in whatever I could find.

After a couple of months, I went back to the VA to apply to the school in New Hampshire. Amanda and I took Kylie to New Hampshire on long day trips to see what country living was like while waiting for the paperwork to get through the VA. We visited the school in its idyllic country setting and beautiful colonial-inspired buildings. Amanda and I loved it and decided to look for an apartment. We didn't wait for the final word from the VA. We were confident we wanted to move north of Rhode Island and settle in New Hampshire.

Amanda and I discussed all our options. We considered the distance between Rhode Island and New Hampshire, and West Virginia, our ability to visit relatives, and vice versa. Amanda thought of the quality of education Kylie would receive and how far from 'civilization' we might be. When the VA approved my request, and the college accepted my application, we settled in Antrim, N.H., a small, old town as quaint as any in New England. The college was located only a couple of miles away. It was perfect. Everything about the college, the town, the neighborhood, the people struck me as ideal. Amanda got into the 'backwoods,' laid-back atmosphere prevalent in NH, and her adjustment met with a great deal of approval. We found a second-floor apartment two houses away from the Catholic church. Everything was falling into place. Now we had to make the most use of the time we had left in Rhode Island and begin packing our things for the move north.

Amanda kept working while I packed up our belongings. I was glad I had help from Mom and my sisters. My dad and my brothers helped us pack a truck and three cars for the journey to our new home. Amanda gave her boss notice just before we left. She gave him our new address, and he said he would mail up her last paycheck. The old-fashioned comfort was perfect for Kylie and Amanda, and I was happy for both of them.

Finding work for Amanda was easy; she located a secretarial position in a firm close by. The last secretary had recently retired, and Amanda had the skills the company needed, so she got the job. She now felt complete and satisfied.

When I wasn't in school, I needed to find work. It was difficult finding an employer willing to hire a man with one leg. Insurance Company regulations prohibited companies from taking unnecessary risks. The only jobs I was offered were at the bottom.

The job wasn't glamorous by any means, but it was steady, and I had to be good to avoid producing knives that couldn't pass inspection and before being shipped to the customer. of the pay scale, offering no chance of advancement or a decent raise. I searched for work with many different firms and settled on one firm that made knives. The money was satisfactory, but I found more important was the relationship I developed with the man who trained me to create and sharpen the blades. I looked forward to going to work every day and watching Bill Harrison ply his craft.

Bill Harrison was a born-in-the-wood man, right from the sod of New Hampshire. He hunted and fished all over, showed me how to tie a fly, and how to hunt the critters that invaded his garden every year. He would even hunt turtles for their meat. More than once, Bill would bring snapper sandwiches for lunch. He offered me half a sandwich once; I accepted it and enjoyed it. From the old saw, "It doesn't taste like chicken," he said.

"Nope, it doesn't," I replied. I truly enjoyed working with Bill. He invited us to his farm in the country, and we had a fun time exploring 'his' woods and learning those things only old farmers know. He showed Kylie some of the old tools he stowed away in the barn and how to use them. It was an excellent education for all of us, and we shared fine meals with Bill and his wife, Louise. They were a fine couple.

Kylie, Amanda, and I enjoyed the change of moving north and "living in the woods," as my brothers liked to say. During a visit home after six months, the first thing they said was, "Bob, you have an accent."

"You're crazy," I told him. I made it a point to be more careful with my dialect. I never noticed a change in my accent, but the folks I met in Antrim certainly heard my non-New Hampshire accent. I didn't want to make that kind of change to my personality too apparent or too rapid.

College ended after only a year. The VA told me they wouldn't allow me to continue because I didn't have a Private Pilot's license. That was something they missed telling me during my application interview. Thank you, VA. My schooling was heavy with science subjects, and I love science, but I wasn't going to go the route the VA suggested, become a science teacher. At the time, teachers in any field were a dime-a-dozen, and it didn't make sense to go to college to be a teacher if you can't get work after you graduate. So, it was back in the job market for me again.

Amanda got pregnant again, and we had to decide what we were going to do. The apartment wasn't going to house four of us comfortably after the baby was born. I had to look for both a house we could afford and a job to help us pay for it. Newspaper listings pointed to an inexpensive home in Keene, about 30 miles away; at the same time, a manufacturer in Keene was offering opportunities to new hires. We took advantage of both. The house came up first, and we could scrape enough to pay the mortgage for the first two months. It was a HUD house, so no down payment was required. Simple and small, it had all the room we needed to grow our family and still have room Amanda and I needed for ourselves.

The job came a close second, but only because Congress finally passed the Americans with Disabilities Act, the ADA. The new law forced companies across the nation, big and small, to hire individuals with disabilities. I didn't like calling myself disabled or even considered myself handicapped. It was all just a minor inconvenience, a phrase I would use many times.

This new ADA Law was the ticket I needed to get a job, and it worked. I found an easy factory job, the pay, more than adequate, and the situation at home made better. Our second child, Kathleen, was born in September, the first year of my new job. She was not the colicky baby Kylie was; in fact, she was quite the opposite. Amanda and I could sleep all night without interruption, but Kathy was a hungry baby. I was beginning to think we bore a factory from what she would eat and shit so many times a day. We were beginning to think there was something wrong with her.

In a couple of years, though, Amanda got pregnant again, and it wasn't an easy time for either of us. She was appalled having to go through the whole 9-month thing again. She hated it the first time with Kylie, the second time with Kathy, and now she was making the atmosphere in the house unbearable because she was pregnant again. But it wasn't all her fault. My hours at work were giving us no social life, not on the outside, not together. I wouldn't count her getting pregnant as 'social time.' As is said, 'shit happens,' and when it does, Amanda hates it; carrying the baby, the labor pains, the birth, it made her very unhappy, a bit depressed. I was happy we would have another child and hoped it would be a boy, but it didn't matter. I enjoyed the company of my children, maybe more than she did.

Amanda gave me the feeling our marriage was falling apart after Anna Lee was born. She forced me to act in a way I did not approve. Waiting to take her home from the hospital, she said, point-blank,

"You either get a vasectomy, or I get my tubes tied. I'm not going through thing again." That 'baseball bat to the gut feeling' came up again. My dreams of a large family, of having a son, were flushed down the toilet. There was nothing I could do. I didn't like what Amanda was asking, and I always hated ultimatums, but I knew I wasn't going to win any arguments against either procedure. I didn't have it in me to put her under the knife, so arrangements were made with my doctor to have the vasectomy. I truly hated doing it.

It was against my religion, my moral principles. That was my conclusion. I talked to my priest about it, but he couldn't, no, he wouldn't, give me the answer I was looking for. He was no help.

"The decision is yours, Bob. The Church can't recommend for or against the procedure."

I had it done, and I hated Amanda for forcing me into it.

"Chivalry is damned," I kept telling myself. "No woman is worth that kind of sacrifice or should ask it of any man."

Amanda and I had our ups and downs after that, and over the years, far too many of them. It was a struggle for me to find any measure of peace with her. She would take the kids out during the day and come home in a pretty good mood, but she wouldn't stay that way when I got home from work. I couldn't figure out why. Sometimes I might do or say something the wrong way, and sometimes she would, and resolution came hard or not at all. Time is supposed to heal all wounds, but boy does it leave a nasty scar.

I will admit I made a few mistakes, but not where forgiveness was out of the question. I guess the worst of any mistake I made was the embarrassment it caused her when I fucked-up in front of her friends. Amanda wanted her life to be proper, in the house and in Society. Damn me if I got in the way. Amanda often found a way to make me pay, but she had her share of fuck-ups as well, yet I never thought I couldn't forgive her.

Like many of the veterans I talked to from WWII, Korea, and Viet Nam, their marriages were like 'sitting on headstones, sometimes.'

After a while, I began seeing the relationship between Amanda and me the same way; she turned cold and hard and didn't want to look down to see whose name was on that stone. We didn't talk much after one blowout, and it didn't matter who was at fault.

She hit her limit one October and asked me to leave the house. Some discussions over it ran hot; other times, it was a cold stare and silence. I couldn't beg for forgiveness; the rope was already around my neck.

Vietnam left me with more souvenirs than the loss of my leg; PTSD was one. It used to be called shell shock or battle fatigue. I had heard of it but didn't think it had caught up with me. I felt fine, I swear! But it found a way in and dug a hole in my soul, leaving wounds I couldn't heal by myself. The more I tried to control my anger, the more it would rage, and Amanda found the right buttons to push, and when to push them. Apologies were never enough, and in front of the kids, all I could do was crawl away and hide.

Two days before Halloween, I left the house leaving the girls devastated. They wanted to come with me, but I had to say no.

"You have to stay with your mother, girls. Daddy has no place to raise you. I don't even have a bed for myself. Where are you going to sleep?"

Like children, they had a solution to every problem, but they didn't understand. I walked away with tears running like a waterfall, my little one tugging on my jacket.

"Go to your mother, Annie, go now. Daddy will see you later." As soon as she turned around, I was in my truck and down the road.

I drove in any direction on the open road and found a motel 5 miles away, The Pillow Talk. It certainly wasn't top-notch, but I wasn't going to be fussy tonight. The receptionist took what I had for a week's rent. My wallet was empty. I didn't have anything for even the simplest meal at McDonald's, but I wasn't feeling all that hungry right now. I had a small, stuffy room, like it hadn't been rented in a while. The bed was made, and the few dishes available were stacked on the shelf. The sink was clean, and there weren't any messes anywhere else in the room. I laughed at my predicament for fear of crying myself out. Looking about the tiny cave, I had a 3 X 4 melamine table on chrome legs and four chrome-legged, padded vinyl chairs. The stove had three burners, a small oven, and a coffee pot. I had a place setting for four in the cupboard and the same silverware serving in one drawer. There weren't any towels, only the linens on the bed. I guessed I was supposed to bring my own.

The fridge was apartment-sized and cold, so I knew it was working. The water in the pipes was hot and cold and clear. It didn't taste too bad, like city water. After surveying the room and getting my bearings, I lay down on the firm mattress and dropped off to sleep. Two hours later, I woke up hungry. I had some change in my pocket and remembered there might be enough change in the truck to purchase a meal. After locking the door to my room, I scoured the truck and,

"Eureka! I found a little more money." I started counting the bills and the change in one of the cup holders.

"Geez! Almost ten bucks. I can eat tonight," I thought.

I got to thinking of my kids, crying themselves to sleep tonight cause their daddy wasn't home; he won't be tucking them in tonight. I won't be tucking them in tonight. The more I thought of it, the angrier I got. I forgot about eating and raced to the house. I banged on the door and waited for her to open it.

Breathing deeply through my anger, I began to calm down. My chest was still heaving when Amanda opened the door.

"Are you crazy?" she asked, "banging on the door like that. The kids are in bed. I had a hell of a job getting them to sleep. And what will the neighbors say? Geez-us Christ!"

"And who's fault is that? I'm the one they wanted to go with, Amanda, not stay with you. You should be the one leaving the house, not me. They're only here because I have no place to raise them, no beds for them to sleep at night. We have to talk about this, Amanda. You can't just drop the hammer on me and expect everything will be alright."

She stood and glared down at me with her arms crossed. The only thing missing was the steam coming out of her ears. I know she heard me, every word. I was sure she was trying to come up with some response. When it came, I was more shocked than when she threw me out a couple of hours ago. She looked at me and said,

"Get yourself a lawyer; we're through. I don't want any more of you."

"Why? "I begged. "Where am I going to go?"

"I, don't, care," she said, "but find a good lawyer. I'm fed up with your PTS… what-ever-you-call-it bullshit. The war was fifteen years ago; put it behind you. I can't deal with these episodes of yours' anymore, Bob. It's driving me out of my mind, and the kids are affected by it. They're hard for me to control sometimes. Your things will be in the garage; you can pick them up anytime, but don't come by without calling first. I might be busy."

Right then, I wished I had died in Viet Nam. She just admitted she had a boyfriend. Every dream, every promise made to one another, exploded, in place, silently, like in Nam. For more than fifteen years, Amanda and I helped each other through some tough times. I helped her get her sanity back when her father passed, and her brother died of the same disease two months later. The kicker was when her mother passed from a heart attack. Amanda felt so all alone; anxiety and depression sent her spinning out of control. She spent three months in a private sanitarium with in-house counseling, away from the kids. Her sister flew in from West Virginia to lend a hand before I lost my mind. Visiting Amanda almost every day and working and the stuff around the house, her sister Kate was a big plus in keeping things together.

Amanda and I watched each other like hawks for almost two years, wondering which of us would fail some sort of testing period.

I tried so hard not to upset her. I didn't want to see her explode again; not only would that be bad for her, but it would be bad for me and indeed bad for the girls. I paid no attention to the possibility that our relationship was in a downhill spiral. Amanda made no signs that things were that bad between us. I didn't see it, but I guess it was Amanda that was sitting on a headstone.

I parked in the driveway the next afternoon to stop and see the girls and try to talk to Amanda. As I got out of my truck, I watched her place two of my suitcases by the door. I ran up and asked her why she was doing this. She didn't have a good answer, or she wouldn't give me one. She only repeated,

"We will discuss how to split things up when we sit down with the lawyers. Now, you can take a thousand from Savings to pay for the lawyer, but not a penny more. I don't want you coming around the house. We can discuss your visits with the kids later." Then she slammed the door shut. I yelled out to her,

"You can't stop me from seeing the girls, Amanda. Amanda!"

I couldn't talk to her; I couldn't get a word in edgewise. I felt lost, in a black hole, and saw no way out. I threw the suitcases in the back of the truck and headed for the only place I could think of that might ease my puzzled mind, the local tavern. There I knew Sam would listen, and he knew how. He was in Nam and went through the same shit I went through. Sam went before the judge during his divorce, and his argument against his wife impressed the court. Sam won a reduction in alimony, so he likes to think he came out on top. He is alone, yes, but he's not lonely. He might be able to give me some advice.

"Hi, Bob," he would say, and that would start a conversation. He knew I was not much of a drinker, and he knew why I was there. "Have another flashback?"

"Yeah," I told him. "A big one." I did not want the other guys in the bar to hear me. Most of them were vets, all from different conflicts. Jack Simons, a former Marine, served in Korea,

"Inchon was a mess," he'd say every time someone asked him, "A big fucking mess."

Today was Friday, and it happened to be Jack Simon's day to be angry.

"MacArthur had it right when he invaded North Korea. It wasn't his fault he got his ass kicked a couple of times. If the goddamn politicians had let him run the war the way generals are supposed to, you wouldn't have that son-of-a-bitch, crazy teenager running the place. I say nuke the whole fucking peninsular." Jack did not forget that MacArthur's invasion at Inchon was a success. But and he never forgot or forgave anyone after losing a younger brother in the invasion.

Bill Henderson served in Korea, also. A jet-jockey, he flew over the Yalu in his Saber jet and took a few hits. Bailing out a few miles north of friendly territory, it took him two weeks to find the American lines and convince them he was an American pilot, uniform and all. Bill's parents are Japanese, and they dropped the Chang in their last name. They took Henderson from a book of names his mother read, waiting to get their citizenship. I guess the G.I.'s and friendly So. Koreans didn't know the difference between an American Henderson and a Japanese Chang. Bill's only comments on the war were his flying prowess and his number of kills. He enjoys telling anyone that he got three red stars painted on the side of his plane.

Jackson Oliver was a black fellow that served in Nam,

It was back in '67, III Corps. In January, Operation Cedar Falls was a massive search and destroy mission. They loaded us up to clean house in the woods, (Hobo Woods) and the Triangle. that was Charlie's playground, and we took it away from him." Jackson knew I was there.

hat's all Jackson would say. Oh, yes, you could press him for more, but only if you wanted to hear a real war story, getting totally fucked-up at the same time. Jackson liked his beer, but I don't think he ever got used to the authentic 6.0 (alcohol %) you buy here in the states. 3.2, watered-down warm piss, was what the Army served us in Nam. It was hard to find the real stuff unless you knew who to see. When you saw Jackson with a beer in his hand, it was wise to take a long way around to your seat.

A few Iraq and Afghanistan vets would come in now and again, but not regularly. Most of the time, they would be thrown out because they could not hold their liquor, and it wasn't just the beer they sought. Overseas, the men drank hard liquor. Jack Daniels was the most popular. The beer was the regular 6.0. Their missions were complex and dangerous; their drinking was commensurate with their mission, and the end result was always destruction; they brought their conflicts home. Sam would not let them back in until they apologized to everyone there, and they had to pay for any damages they caused, including the painting.

An old fellow sipping double rye on ice sat at a corner table by the last window opposite the main entrance. Only Sam knew how old Jimmy Scrolls was because "that's the way Jimmy wants it", Sam would tell us. Every day, Jimmy would walk in, order his double-shot, and sit, dragging his gnarled and crooked fingers through the pages of an old photo album he and his Elizabeth kept over the 67 years they were married. Elizabeth passed away three years ago. Jimmy says she wanted him to promise he would keep that table for her and sit there every day until she came back for him. He served in WWII, Saipan in the Philippines, Korea, and at the beginning of Nam. The Marines forced him out before it got too hot. The Commandant said the Marines could not bear to see an old warhorse go down, either from the weight of his medals or a bullet, so they let him go. A second story goes around that Elizabeth might have had something to do with it. Jimmy shakes his head, "No!"

Sam looked up at me. I slowly sipped the beer I wasn't sure I wanted and said to me,

"Bob. Go over and talk to Jimmy. He understands better than me and certainly better than any of these bozos. Go on. He's looking right at you, for chri-sakes."

I walked over and stood by the edge of the table.

"What are you waiting for, son?" Jimmy asked, right off.

"Have a seat. Do you want to freshen that beer?"

Before I knew it, Sam had a cold stein of Bud on the table in front of me. He patted me on the shoulder and nodded to Jimmy. As Sam went back to the bar, Jimmy asked,

"Having problems at home, son? Your wife asks you to leave the house?" He pulled out a fresh pack of Pall Mall's, tore the seal, and placed one between his cracked, dry lips. Jimmy has got to be near ninety years old, and he's still smoking. He offered me one.

"No, thanks," I said.

He took a long drag and enjoyed it, still, after all these years.

"Yeah, Amanda did all that and more. She told me she found a friend; not to come around without calling first. She said she might be busy." That said, I started to cry quietly

"Go ahead and cry, son. With what you've been through already, crying at the loss of your family is the least you can do."

"I know I have PTSD, the VA told me. They're even willing to pay me for it. But I'm not doing well controlling it. It hurts me, the wife, and my kids. I think they hate me when I erupt. I know their mother does. And I have never hurt her. I have never hurt the kids."

Jimmy dragged on his cigarette as if it helped him think. Then he took and a sip on his whiskey. He raised his hand toward the bar and had Sam bring us another round.

"Your kids don't hate you, son. They just don't know how to understand what you're going through. Your wife doesn't understand, and she's not going to. She can't. She hasn't seen or been through what we've been through."

"I don't have the answers these guys think I have. I just don't approach the problem the same way they do. My wife, God love her, and I had our troubles every time I came home from war, and I made it through more than most men. My wife and me married early and she saw me through every conflict I fought, even my battle with PTSD and drinking. It was hard, son, but love made us both persevere. Love and a lot of talking."

"I have to say, and I believed her, when she said she never had a boyfriend. She never played that card on me. I have to admit I have fallen a couple of times, but Elizabeth forgave me. I didn't deserve it, no man does. To be forgiven after cheating on his wife? What do you think those vows were for? But God sent me an angel and she forgave me, and I ain't never cheated since. Your wife doesn't sound like she cares one way or the other, anymore. My advice is let her go. A woman like that can't be trusted. You're better off without her."

"If that sounds harsh, how harsh is it that she can tell you she's found someone else…Don't come around, I'll be busy." "Those are painful words, deep cuttin' words. They are not said in a moment of anger. The act has already been done. The best thing for you to do now is concentrate on your children. How old are they?"

"Ten, twelve, and fifteen," I told him.

"Don't worry. They'll come around, but you are going to have to be patient with them. As your kids get older, you're going to have to sit them down and tell them what's going on. You're gonna have to do it without anger, not like their mother. I'm sure she's not doing you any good to the children.

Let it be. Get her back in court, on your terms. You're going to have to be generous, not for her, but for your kids. And let her complain all she wants. Do what you can, follow the law, and don't let your children see you fight with her. Avoid it if you can."

Pointing to his heart he said, "In here, and in here." Jimmy said, pointing to his head. "It's all for your kids, nothing for her, not anymore."

"But first, get to work on yourself as soon as you can. I'm not going to tell you that your wife is going to come back to you. From, what you've told me that is not going to happen."

"I've been going to the VA once a week and talking to a guy there. We sit in a group and talk about the war and how we feel today. He talks about this part of the brain, that part of the brain, what was affected, and what might not have been."

"Did this fella show you what his credentials were? Is he a doctor, a psychiatrist? Is he even a counselor specializing in veterans and combat injuries? If not, they can only go so far with you. I don't know, they might be able to help you, but if I were you, I'd make my way to a veteran's outpost in this area that will do a hell of a lot more good than the VA."

I sipped my beer while Jimmy took another drag from his Pall Mall. I glanced his way a couple of times, not sure how to take his advice. Jimmy could feel my hesitant heart and waited for me to say something. He sipped his rye.

Reaching into his front pocket, he pulled out a very worn and ragged wallet, the seams torn and falling apart. It looked as though he carried a library in his back pocket. Jimmy rifled through the separate pieces of paper and found a business card.

"Here," he said, pushing the card across the table to me.

"Call that number and make an appointment with Tony J, the chief counselor, no one else. If he tries to pass you off to another counselor, tell him I sent you. He'll fit you in. You have got to make time to see him. I don't care how busy you think you are; you see him when you are scheduled."

"He can help me save my family?" I asked.

"I'm not sending you there to save your family. I'm sending you there to save your life."

"But..."

"No buts, son. You don't know what you're dealing with. PTSD will kill you. Did the VA tell you that?"

"No." I told him.

"I didn't think so" He snuffed out the stub of the cigarette, took down the last of his rye, and got up to leave.

"I'll be right with you, dear." I heard him say. Then, standing, he fell face first, onto the table and slid off onto the floor, in front of me. Jimmy Scrolls died right before me, right after giving me the best advice I had ever gotten from anyone. It was advice designed to save my life.

Sam ran from behind the bar and yelled out,

"Somebody call 9-1-1."

He carefully turned Jimmy over and listened for a heartbeat. He heard nothing and immediately began mouth to mouth and chest compressions. Thirty seconds went by, one minute, another 30 seconds, and Jimmy didn't stir. Sam continued with the life-saving techniques he had learned as a Corpsman in Viet Nam.

Just then, Dr. Maurice Alcott walked in, as was his routine every Friday. He saw the crowd gathered around someone lying on the floor. He immediately recognized it was Jimmy Scrolls.

Excused, me, Sam." he said, giving Sam a tap on the shoulder. He began a cursory examination of Jimmy.

How long have you been at this? he asked, looking at Sam.

About three minutes, Doc. An ambulance is on the way."

I think it's too late, looking up at us.

He took his last sip of whiskey, I told them, then said, "I'll be right with you, dear." Then he stood up and fell over. I just sat there, stunned; I didn't know what to do.

When the ambulance arrived, the EMTs went to work. Doc got up to address one of them. The EMT placed an oxygen mask on Jimmy and took his blood pressure. They tried to talk to Jimmy. I don't know if they got an answer or not. Placing Jimmy on the gurney, they loaded him into the ambulance and drove away with the obligatory siren wailing.Sam looked at me, standing there, stunned at what happened in front of me.

Doc Alcott asked, Are you okay, son?

"Yeah, I'm okay. I've seen guys get hit in Nam. Some died, some didn't. But I never saw anyone just drop-dead right in front of me.

Let me tell you something about Jimmy Scrolls.

We took a seat at the bar, and Doc ordered two beers.

Thanks, Doc. Mind if I call you, Doc?

Everyone else does, he said and offered his hand, Dr. Maurice Alcott, GP.

I offered mine in return. Bob Lafond, fucked-up, Vet.

We all are, son. Isn't that what the general public wants to think of us? Especially those of us that served in Nam.

Yeah, I guess. sighing deeply.

So, Doc went on. Let me tell you a bit of Jimmy Scrolls."

We both sipped our beers.

Jimmy served in WWII, Korea, and the onset of Nam. He was a machine gunner in all three theaters: first in line, point, on patrol. You can see I'm not old enough to have served on Saipan alongside Jimmy, but I did get to see him come home from Korea. Fact is, I treated Jimmy and gave him the okay to go to Nam. So, I've known him a few years."

When Jimmy came home from his short stay in Nam, he told me of the things he saw. He was suffering inside, saying he had enough. I asked him how I could help. He told me he wanted to talk to somebody. He needed to speak to somebody. He was having nightmares and thrashing out in his dreams, with Elizabeth laying there next to him. I gave him the name of an excellent psychiatrist and counselor I knew. He went to see the guy and then came back to see me six months later. He thanked me, profusely, saying,

You helped save my marriage, Doc, he said, and he went away. I saw Jimmy again 12 years later. He searched me out and came to my office. Again, it was the nightmares, and this time his wife was threatening to leave him. I could see the desperation in his eyes, and hers'. I gave him the name of the man on that card Jimmy gave you.

Did it help?

Elizabeth came to see me and said thank you, that that man saved their marriage. When she was on her deathbed, it was Jimmy who asked me to look in on her. That's when she said to me the exact words she told her husband. The same last words you heard him say when he stood up. Jimmy thought Elizabeth had come back for him, that he saw her calling him. He stood up and went with her when he died, right there. We all want to die like Jimmy Scrolls, son, with a woman who will stand by us to the end. She will see and feel every sin we could ever commit and still call us home at the end of the day. She'll be the only friend you'll have when the whole world has given up on you. Jimmy knew that, his wife knew that, and that's how he came to see her in the end."

I was stunned at the story, almost wishing the same thing would happen to Amanda and me. I looked at Doc, said thanks for the beer, and got up to leave. Sam looked at me,

"Jimmy gave you good advice, Bob. follow it, right, Doc?" Sam interjected.

"Sam is right, Bob. As veterans, after combat, we need a different kind of medicine. Here's your chance to take advantage of a specialized kind that will make a big difference in your life. Ask any of these fellas. Jimmy was right all the time. Good night, son."

Doc offered his hand, we shook, and I left.

CHAPTER 28

Thinking Alone

It was almost two miles back to the house. A shuttle bus went by every two hours and stopped to ask if I wanted a ride. I said no, I needed the walk. The weather was good, conducive for a stroll, but mine wasn't going to be very enjoyable. Too much thinking was going into this walk. I'll have to think this out and make all the right decisions, the first being to see Tony J. and get the help I need.

I thought of all Jimmy had said, but I could not get the picture of his death right in front of me out of my head. He saw his wife or thought he did and was ready to go with her. To where? Heaven? Maybe. Wherever. He just dropped dead. I started to shake and reached into my pocket for a cigarette, for the moment forgetting that I had given up smoking two months ago.

I stopped in my tracks and had to think, where am I? Where was I going? What was going on in my head? I saw a drug store across the street, so I stopped in for a pack of cigarettes. The first match wouldn't strike. It took the second match three times, and it didn't light. The third match lit on the first strike.

"Nerves," I said aloud. I bought a soda and a Twinkie and walked down to the church. I sat on one of the foundation stones near the walkway. I was there twenty minutes when Fr. Michael came walking around the corner. I turned my head, hoping he wouldn't recognize me. Too late.

"Hi, Bob," he said.

"Hello, Father," I acknowledged him with a halfhearted smile.

"What brings you by the church this time of night, Bob?" the priest asked as he sat on the stone next to me.

I took a drag on my cigarette and looked up at him, saying,

"Amanda asked me to leave the house."

Fr. Michael's pause was as loud as a cannon shot.

"I'm sorry to hear that, Bob. Do you want to tell me why?"

"Sure," and I took a sip of my drink.

I went through the whole story. He knew of Nam and our early life, coming to New Hampshire, college, and jobs again. He knew the kids, and he remembered us, as a family, in church on Sunday mornings. But he didn't know of the PTSD and the things I had done that piled up.

"She said she has met someone and has been seeing him for a while. She said she's tired of dealing with me in and out of hospitals, dealing with my PTSD bullshit...those are her words, father."

I went on for more than an hour, through three cigarettes, the Twinkie, and my drink. I got up twice to warm my ass from the cold, granite stones.

I expected Fr. Michael to say something, do something, but he just sat there listening to my story. I hoped he was listening. I didn't know. I stood up and stared in numbed silence. He just sat there. I shook my head and began walking away. Fr. Michael asked,

"Where are you going, Bob?"

"Well, you're so quiet, Father; I thought you had fallen asleep," I told him.

"Not on these cold stones, Bob, not on these stones."

"No, I was taking in your story trying to find an answer for you."

"There is no answer, Father. Not this time. The way things kept piling up over the years, Amanda not willing to talk or see a counselor, I had a feeling the end was just around the corner. It didn't matter to her anymore what I tried to do to make amends. She had already made up her mind. Then I find out why; a boyfriend."

I put out my cigarette and said, "I'm going back to my motel room. I don't know how long I'm going to stay there. I still have the girls to worry about and find a lawyer. I may come in sometime and talk about an annulment. I'll see where things go. Good night, Father."

"Good night, Bob," Father said.

I walked back to my truck; the bar was closed. I sat in the cab, the neon Bud sign in the bar's window drowning my windshield in red light. I lit another cigarette and headed for the motel. It didn't matter to the manager what time I got back. I had my key.

My room was at the end of a string of 12 cottages, all the same. A blue neon sign, out front, told the world this shit hole motel existed and flashed onto my bed all night. The on-off-on-off, hypnotic pulse fixed itself in my brain and had me rolling all night. The only sleep I got came after I buried my head under the pillow. At least there weren't any noises accompanying the sign.

The rising sun, burning through my window and into my eyelids, forced me into a cold shower. A look at the clock told me I had to hurry. I was on duty for the morning shift at work, and it would not look good for the boss to see me add dirt on my perfect record. I wished he would buy me a coffee for once. That would make it so much easier for both of us to say good morning.

After finishing my shift, I decided to stop by the house and see the girls. By noon on a Saturday, I knew Kylie and Kate would be up and dressed, but Anna Lee might still be in her pajamas. Amanda should be up and had her second cup of coffee. I knocked on the door and saw her looking down at me. She was not pleased to see me.

"What do you want, Bob?"

"I came to see the girls, and you cannot stop me without a court order, and that you will never get," I told her. I said, straight out, she was wrong in her assertions and conclusions about my behavior.

With a momentary lapse in her assault, she turned and called to the girls, "Your father is here."

Kylie and Kate jumped up and came to the door, bursting by their mother, strangling me with their hugs.

"Where's your sister?"

"She's getting dressed," Kate said.

"She'll be right down," added Kylie.

No sooner said than done, Anna Lee was there, right by my side. "Are you coming home soon, dad?" Anna asked.

"Why don't you get your coats, and we'll go for a ride and talk about that."

They piled into the truck, and off we went. Amanda was not pleased the girls wanted, so willingly, to come with me. I drove to a donut shop for hot cocoa and a donut. I wanted to talk to the girls, but not in a public setting. There was a small park not far from the house. The girls ran to the bench where we sat and drank our cocoa.

"Are you and mommy getting a divorce?" Kylie asked. Kate and Anna were looking straight into my face waiting for my answer. I took a deep breath and told them,

"It looks like that's what your mother wants."

"But why?" asked Kate.

I had no answer that made sense to me; how would I explain it to my daughters.

"Well," I paused, sighing. "I guess daddy may have made a few mistakes, and your mother isn't in the mood to forgive them. Sometimes married people get tired of each other, things go wrong, and there's no way to fix it. They decide divorce is the best way."

I bit my tongue with every word, not wanting to blame Amanda for her confessed infidelity. I didn't know how stable the family unit would be from now on, but my heart was broken that I wasn't going to be part of the unit anymore.

Anna Lee looked up at me with giant tears running down her cheeks. She told me there were kids in her school whose parents were divorced and had a new mommy or daddy living in their houses. She didn't want a new daddy living in her house. She wanted me. I couldn't hold it in any longer. I grabbed the three of them and hugged them close and cried with them in my arms. We stayed that way for more than a minute. Kylie looked into my eyes and said,

"I love you, daddy." Kate followed with, "Me, too," and Anna Lee, with "Me, too."

I told them, "No matter how this turns out, I always want you to behave for your mother. I don't want you to blame her for anything. Daddy will be around when you need me, and I will help you out whenever you ask. If your mother finds a new friend, you have to be nice and polite. If he moves into the house, you must still behave."

The silence that followed was frightening. I didn't know what the girls would do next. Then, Anna ran to the swings, calling me to give her a push. Kate and Kylie soon followed. It was a change of heart that only a ten-year-old could bring.

We stayed in the park for almost three hours. It was exhausting but fun. I truly enjoyed being with them. I didn't know how many more times I would be allowed to take them like this. I brought them home with smiles on their faces, reserved smiles, but they were happy to have had the time with their father.

Amanda didn't come to the door to greet the kids or me, but I wasn't expecting her to. I watched them enter the house, Anna Lee turning to wave goodbye and blow a kiss. I blew one back to her and quickly turned to the truck. The girls were in the window waving goodbye as I drove away, with tears in my eyes.

The girls and I kept a visitation routine every other week, but I didn't want to set a schedule for them. They needed space to do the things they like to do with their friends. I needed time, too. I called a lawyer and made an appointment to stop by his office. After he took five hundred dollars out of my pocket, we discussed how to proceed in my best interest and the best interest of the girls. Neither he nor I could care less of Amanda's interest. I told him what I wanted to do.

"I want this over as fast as possible." I made my pitch, but he explained no matter what I wanted, it all had to be presented to Amanda and her lawyer before there were any agreements.

CHAPTER 29

The Last Mind Scramble

The whole divorce thing was really messing with my mind. I was making mistakes at work, missing time because I was sleeping in late. There was no desire to spend time with friends even though there were other 'friends' they wanted me to meet. I wasn't ready for all that new friend thing. Girls were the farthest thing from my mind. I was worried about my three kids.

Calling Amanda to make arrangements to see the children was a hassle. I hated making the phone call, but it was the only time she would talk to me. Driving up to the house, I hoped the kids were outside playing. That way, I could see them and not get bothered by their mother. Oh, how I hated bumping into her. I tried to be civil at all times to avoid conflict and show the kids 'daddy can be nice.'

Amanda was a pain in the ass about the whole thing. She wanted my ass on a silver platter, leaving as little as possible for me to live on. I knew my pension from work was up for grabs, but I was content knowing she could not touch my disability check. Her salary from work made my payment to her much more bearable.

Within a couple of months, we had our appointment with the judge. Then I got to see Amanda's boyfriend. She must have brought him along for support, or advice, or something. It didn't work. In the end, she huffed about the settlement, but both her lawyer and mine and the judge told me I was more than generous in the settlement.

The Decree of Divorce became official in March, so I went to see Fr. Michael and applied for an annulment. He and I discussed the critical aspects of the dissolution and what I had to do when the form arrived. He told me it would come in the mail, and Amanda would also get one. The paper had questions about every year of our marriage. The honesty flowed like water. I held nothing back and didn't have to make anything up. Amanda refused to fill them out. She assumed, following the annulment, that our children would be declared illegitimate. I laughed at her ignorance and explained how wrong her conclusion was. It didn't matter whether she filled out the papers or not. When my annulment came through, it would apply to her also. It took a year for it all to be finalized, and I felt good about being able to marry in the Church again if I wanted to.

It's always said that time heals all wounds. Maybe, but the scars left behind can be nasty ones. There were times spent being reckless, from Nam to today, but in the end, I learned always to be careful when you're walking through cemeteries and never look down when you're sitting on a headstone.

END

Oath Of Enlistment To The Uniformed Services

I, (NAME), do solemnly swear (or affirm) that I will support and defend the Constitution of the United States against all enemies, foreign and domestic; that I will bear true faith and allegiance to the same; and that I will obey the orders of the President of the United States and the orders of the officers appointed over me, according to regulations and the Uniform Code of Military Justice. So help me, God.

"The apocalypse of any war leaves one to recognize why you never look down when you're sitting on a headstone."

— Robert E. Lafond

THANK YOU'S

Firstly, I want to thank my wife, the rock of our marriage. It was a blessing when you chased me around town and made me smile when you caught me.

Secondly, I need to thank my children, my girls, for their spontaneity, laughter, and strength of love.

Thirdly, to mom and Dad. You taught me well. God Bless You.

Fourth, to my veteran friends, for helping me to keep going in my counseling, crying, and healing.

Fifth, to the doctors and nurses of the 12th Evacuation Hospital on base at the 25th Infantry Battalion

Sixth, To Chili Rokes…I owe you one, buddy.

About The Author

Born on Veterans Day in 1947, the calendar marked the path Bob would take in life, military service. The second of nine children, his mother and father taught Bob and his brothers and sisters to be creative in the face of near poverty. His mother stretched every dollar his father brought home from his two jobs. Bob learned to apply the same level of dedication to everything he did growing up.

Despite a disability he worked 30 years for the US Postal Service, putting three daughters through college. His hobbies are singing Barbershop harmony for the past 27 years and writing poetry and short stories. He and his wife enjoy traveling, having camped across the United States, and traveled abroad. A second book of politics and patriotism is planned for release this Summer.